CHASING *THE HORIZON*

The Dawn of Pandora

L O U I S   L E E

ISBN 978-1-0980-3418-4 (paperback)
ISBN 978-1-0980-3419-1 (digital)

Christian Faith Publishing, Inc.
832 Park Avenue
Meadville, PA 16335
www.christianfaithpublishing.com

Printed in the United States of America

Dedication

James Daniel Boback "Danny"
1984-2016

I would like to dedicate this book to my nephew Danny Boback. His light in this world was brief but it burned brighter than the sun. There is no one way to define him. He was highly intelligent and could retain and incorporate any information that he came across in any situation or conversation. A scollard athlete in football, and in all the sports he played I can't think of anything he didn't accomplish. Most importantly of all he was a God conscious man with a truly caring heart. He would humorously refer to me as his "crazy uncle." We had a lot of fun with the, back and forth, that came from that title and I wear it proudly to this day. I silently knew him as a "prince."

Acknowledgment

I would like to offer a heartfelt thank you to everyone who offered their thoughts and/or insights in one way or another. I asked a select number of people to read this book and give me their feedback. And while it got handed off to more, all of the names listed below did give me their opinions and my conversations with them were not only encouraging but vital to know I was on the right track. There names are as follows.

I would like to thank, GOD!

I would also like to thank,

Charlene R. Lee (Mom)	Brandon Julian Lee (My boy)	Sally Su Lee
Diann Lee	Debbie Lee Boback	Kevin Gerstner
Austin Lee	John L. Cox	Bill Halloran
Trisha Valentine	Kathy and Stephen Vash	Hal Snellgrose
Jessie Teschker	Gene and Jeanette Esposito	Don Crowther

Casi Dickery

Ashley Henderson

Colleen Schumann

Debra Purcell Collins

Jennifer Collaton (Pheobe)

Chris Wittaker

Jan Conzelmann

Peter Jensen

Lea Goodfellow

Jennifer FitzGerald

Deanna M. Donnelly

Ali Swindoll

Melinda Lewis and Betty Sue (Pooch)

Edward Gulliver and Anna Malawski

Debbie Turnbull-Swindlehurst

Leigh Ann Purcell

Steve and Brabara Willard

Mike and Laraine Fountain

Jennifer Lockwood-Krenson

Melissa Jensen

Sandy Nadreau

Amy Barack

Robert Fox III

Paul Braid

Joe Rushworth

Andrea Tambling

Dianna Whitney

Helen Beller

Robert K. Myers

Tony Pizza

Tom Tarantelli

Kathy Arbelo

Dillon Martino

Jessica Laing

Listed below are the names of those who influenced verbiage or factual content.

Charlene R. Lee (Mom)

Brandon Julian Lee (My boy)

Sally Su Lee

Trisha Valentine   John L. Cox   Edward
                                       Gulliver

Melinda Lewis   Robert Graettinger Leigh Ann
                                       Purcell

Jennifer Collaton Jennifer
(Phoebe)   Lockwood-Krenson

In addition there were a few who expressed a need for or inspired an expansion of a story line within the book, so I would like to offer them further acknowledgement.

Brandon Julian   Sally Su Lee   Jennifer
Lee (My boy)   Collaton
                                       (Phoebe)

Jennifer   Leigh Ann Purcell
Lockwood-
Krenson

    A special thanks to my friend and fellow author, Mike Houston. I told him my idea for this book and he encouraged me to move forward with it. Had that not happened I'm not sure that I would have ever gotten around to writing "Chasing the Horizon, the Dawn of Pandora."

Chapter *1*

The Hand of Fate

Just outside of the southeast portion of Indianapolis, Indiana, lies a small town called Beech Grove, and just outside of the southeast portion of Beech Grove on a section of Highway 40 lies a small, local hometown grocery called Bobba Lou's. It sits among a sparse number of houses just before the seemingly unending rows of cornfields that follow farther to the south.

Bobba Lou's is owned and operated by a good-natured, portly man named Lou, short for Louis, who is most often clad in overalls. He became owner of the grocery after his Uncle Bob had passed away. His Uncle Bob was affectionately known as Bobba, a nickname that stayed with him after the mispronunciation that Lou had made of his uncle's name when he was just a toddler. Instead of calling him Bob, he would say, "Bobba," so the name stuck. It was Bobba's Grocery until Bobba died, and then after that, it became Bobba Lou's.

It seemed that most everything that involved the grocery store was in the hands of Lou himself from taking out the trash to stocking the shelves, from taking inventory and even butchering the meats, which he did three days a week on Mondays, Wednesdays, and Fridays. He would carve up the whole portions that were delivered there and then take the scraps in a large garbage can to the Dumpster out in the back parking lot.

Well, this summer morning was far different than most any other. As he was unloading the scraps into the Dumpster, he noticed what looked like a fallen, fleshy piece of meat about twenty yards away. Curious, he thought, *How could it have gotten so far away from the Dumpster? Maybe an animal, perhaps.* As Lou approached, he realized that it was a human hand. Although he was used to the sight of blood and so forth, he was shocked. This was quite different as it was not part of an animal.

Lou quickly backed away and ran back into the grocery store to call the local sheriff's department. After placing the call, Deputy John Lane Scott, a regular patron in Lou's grocery and also a good friend, was dispatched. Lou made his way back out to the parking lot to stand guard over his gruesome discovery.

It was a warm morning, not unusual for that time of year. The sunlight had just begun to crest the earth and was casting long shadows from the dotted trees that surrounded the grocery. The smell in the air was a mixture of Dumpster materials and the sweet smell of the cornfields not far away. "What's taking them so long?" Lou said to himself. In actuality, it had only been about five minutes or so, but for Lou, seemed more like an hour. He wiped sweat from the back of his neck and forehead with a handkerchief that he always kept in his front pocket.

Finally he could see the flash of red-and-blue lights reflecting off the trees in the distance as the police car made its way around to the back of the grocery where Lou had told them he would be. The patrol car made its way in Lou's direction, slowed, and then stopped. Exiting the car was the driver, Deputy Scott, and his partner Mike Nichols. Deputy Scott closed the patrol-car door, then pushed up his policeman's cap with his right thumb. Gesturing in Lou's direction as he used both hands to give a slight tug up of his trousers, he asked, "So what do we have here, Lou? What's going on?"

Lou replied, "Well, I was hoping you could tell me," as he pointed in the direction of his unsightly find. "I was just taking out the morning's refuse when I saw that right over there. Before I had gotten a closer look at it, I thought it was some sort of prank, you know, like from one of those Halloween-type stores."

The two deputies sauntered over and squatted down for a closer look. "Yep, that's the real deal all right. That's a human hand," said Deputy Scott.

Then Mike said, "I'll go get the camera."

"Yeah, we're going to need some shots of this before we bag it. So what else can you tell me about this?"

As he turned toward Lou, Lou scratched his forehead and replied, "Not much else, I'm afraid. I know about as much as you do!"

Scott knelt down for a closer look and noticed there wasn't very much blood for this type of injury. He leaned in even closer and noticed the wound had burn marks where the hand had been severed, almost as though it had been cauterized.

After about forty-five minutes of meticulous investigation, the paramedics were then given instructions to take the hand to the medical examiner's office as they had no role in saving life here. They were simply transporting a body part.

Deputy Scott then shook Lou's hand saying, "Well, my friend, I'll let you know as soon as I find out anything about this, as much as I can anyway. In the meantime, I believe my wife is coming in tomorrow for some of those special cutlets you make for us."

"You bet," Lou said. "I always set 'em aside and have 'em ready for ya."

"You have a great day now," Scott replied. "We'll talk to you soon."

* * * * *

Three days later, down at the police station, Deputy Scott sat at his desk with his feet up on top and was leaning back with a Rubik's Cube in his hand. He held it up as one of the other officers passed by and said, "How the hell do you do one of these things? I've never been able to figure it out." His phone rang. Taking his feet off the desk, he leaned forward and answered it.

"Twenty-third Substation, Deputy Scott here. How can I help you?" It was the medical examiner's office informing him to come in and that they had a full report ready about the severed hand. Fingerprints were identified. They were that of a local man. Scott found this very intriguing. No one had reported anyone injured at a hospital nor had anyone shown up dead or missing anywhere.

* * * * *

A while later when Sheriff Scott was off duty, he stopped in at Bobba Lou's. Scott opened the squeaky screen door of the grocery. He walked across the wooden floor toward the counter where Lou was bagging some groceries for an elderly regular, saying to her, "Is that all, Bonnie?" as Sheriff Scott gave a quick wave, not one of a greeting or a "How do you do?" but more of an "I'm here" short kind of wave.

Lou nodded in Sheriff Scott's direction and then turned his attention back toward Bonnie saying, "Is there anything else I can get for you today?"

"No," she replied. "Lou, you always take real good care of me. Thanks," she said with a smile.

Sheriff Scott was looking down at the ground as the elderly woman made her way toward the exit door. He gave a quick look around the grocery store to see if anyone else was there and then looked back down at the floor until he heard the screen door close.

"Well, hey, Scott. I can tell by the look on your face that this isn't an average visit, is it?" The look on Scott's face was one of puzzlement and concern.

"You're a perceptive man, Lou. It's not the average visit. I got some information about the hand, and listen." He paused for a moment then said, "I can't share all of the information I have, but you've been a good friend for a long time, and I feel I can trust you with some of what we've turned up. Seems you're owed that much as you're the one who found the hand. I can trust you, right?"

Lou nodded his head. "Of course you can. It's been on my mind. It's not every day you find a hand in your parking lot."

Scott said, "Well, after the medical examiner did a full forensic, the burn marks that severed the hand itself weren't like anything that they had ever seen before. It was like a laser-precision cut, only it was different. There were microscopic marks all moving parallel in the same direction.

"The medical examiner said that he had never seen a burn that was anything like it and then did some research and found nothing that matched. So that was the first thing that was really odd. The second thing was that the fingerprints were identified, and it's a local man. I obviously can't say who. I've said too much already even though I know you'll keep this a secret, right?" Scott said again. Lou nodded in reply.

Scott continued, "We went to the address of the identified to find out what happened to him. See if we could find someone there that knew him or could help fill in the blanks. Well, the thing about it is, the man that answered the door was the man whose fingerprints were identified."

"You're kidding me."

"No, and here's the kicker. Are you ready for this? The guy had both hands."

"What?" Lou said. "What do you mean he had both hands? That's crazy. How could that...oh wait, I see, he's a twin, right? He's a twin?"

Scott said, "No. We did a full investigation all the way back to this man's birth, and he was not a twin, and even if he was, twins don't have the exact same fingerprints, even if they're identical twins. It's…it's got us pretty well… We don't know what the hell is going on. We're all as confused as crap. We have nothing more to go on from this point. And to make it even more awkward, we couldn't even tell him about what we found or even why he was being questioned. I tell ya, Lou, in all of my years, I've never seen anything like this. We have no explanation for who this hand belongs to even though we have fingerprints and DNA that says we do. How in the hell do you produce a third hand? It's just crazy. It casts the mind to wonder things like mad scientists and government conspiracies. It's the craziest thing I've ever come across."

Lou said, "You're not having me on, are you?"

"No, actually, I'm not!"

"Oh, come on, really?"

"No, no, I'm not, Lou. It really is a dead-end investigation of a man who apparently has both hands, yet we discovered one of his own. Well, obviously not his hand but one that identically matches his. It's like something out of a sci-fi movie."

"All right," Lou said. "I'll have to try and digest that one," as he scratched his head. "So what now? What are you guys gonna do with this case now?"

"That's the thing. It's pretty much a dead end. We have no idea what to make of it, what to do about it, how to follow up. It's a complete dead end."

"Well, Scott, I have to tell ya. I'm bewildered. I mean, really. You know, if you don't find out anything more about this, it's going to be one of those things that leaves a man wondering all the rest of his days. Thanks for the mystery!"

"Yeah, well, maybe that's another reason why I shared it with you so I don't have to go it alone. But really, if you need to share it with anybody else, share it back with me, or else I'm going to get in trouble for it." Scott took a deep breath. "Now I've got to get moving on down the road. I just wanted to stop in for a few minutes." He looked up at the clock. "Yep, I've got to go. Take care now."

"You too," Lou replied.

FIFTEEN YEARS EARLIER

Bobba, owner of Bobba's Grocery, is in his midsixties. He's been weathered by the years with wrinkles around his eyes and mouth and a drooping chin, not uncommon for a man his age. He has a bulbous nose with tiny, little veins, sort of like Winston Churchill. His hands are leatherlike, thick and worn from years of hard work.

He is loved by the town, always has a smile on his face, and is gracious and kind to every customer. No matter who they are, he treats them as though they're a brother or sister. He has a truly good heart. It's just his way.

Bobba knows most everyone who comes in but is particularly proud of one sixteen-year-old boy named Julian Phillips who has been coming to the grocery with his mom since he was a little boy. He has a soft spot for Julian because Julian's father, Gabe, whom Bobba knew well, passed away many years ago. Today he was picking up some hamburger and some mushroom soup for his mother for the evening's dinner. Bobba looked at Julian and said, "Is that going to be all for you today, Julian?"

"Yes, sir, that's all I've got money for."

"No problem. How's school coming along? You still making straight As?"

"Oh, yes, sir, Mr. Bobba, I sure am. I just got a book on quantum physics. I'm halfway through it."

"Quantum physics? How do you make any sense of that kind of stuff?"

"Well, I really find it fascinating. I can't put the book down."

"What's it about?"

"Well, it's about string theory, wormholes, space-time distortions…things like that."

"What does a worm's hole have to do with quantum physics?" Bobba asked, rather baffled.

"No, no. You don't understand. It's not a worm's hole that's made by a worm. It's a shift. It's a warp in space."

"What do you mean a warp in space?"

"Well, it's kind of like a hole in space that leads from one point to another or from one dimension to another or one time in space to another."

"I don't understand because that doesn't make any sense at all," Bobba continued. "How can nothingness, because space is nothing, how can nothingness have a hole in it? I mean, a hole in something that's not even there? Doesn't make any sense."

With a laugh, Julian said, "Well, I could explain it to you if you've got an hour or two, or I could just loan you my book, and you could figure it out for yourself."

"No, I don't need to read anything about that. Only hole I'm concerned about is the one in my wallet."

Julian grinned and said, "That's a funny one, Bobba. Hey, tell Louis I said hello," as he scooped up the groceries into his arm as though he were carrying a football.

"You're a good boy, Julian. Tell your mama I said hi. And by the way, don't forget me when you're famous someday."

"Oh, I won't," Julian replied. "Now all I have to do is get famous," he said as he clambered out the door.

Bobba extended a forefinger over his lips, saying to himself, "That boy is going to be something someday, something real special. Never seen anybody like him in my life. Sharp as a tack he is."

* * * * *

There were two steps that led from the screen door of the grocery to the parking lot which Julian avoided with a single jump straight down and a short skip to his bicycle waiting nearby. He dropped the groceries into the basket and threw his leg over the seat. And off he went on his tattered, old bike.

Most of his friends by now were at least driving junky, old cars but not Julian. His mom didn't have money like that. As a single mother, she struggled to pay the bills after her husband had died when Julian was in preschool. He never had a clear image of his father, just some vague memories that he had here and there but nothing that he could grasp onto and say, "Yeah, I remember when my dad said this" or "I remember when we did that."

He rode the pale-green, fenderless, wide-tired bicycle, making his way down a side road to an offshoot from the main highway called Lockwood Drive and then down an old, cobbled driveway that led up to a tattered, old house. Time and seasons had taken its toll on the old place. In the last few yards leading up to the house, Julian, while still riding, switched his right leg over the seat so that both feet were on the same pedal as he stood on one side of the bicycle, balancing himself as it coasted to a stop, and then he hopped off.

Laying the bicycle slightly on its side against the porch rail, he grabbed the groceries from the basket and made his way in through the front door. His mother was waiting for him in the kitchen. She was a slender woman with mostly dark hair, speckled with touches of gray, an equally slender nose, high cheekbones, and soft, gentle round eyes that matched her soft, gentle round chin.

As Julian unpacked the groceries, his mother gazed at him with adoring eyes. He was the center of her universe. She had never gotten over the death of her husband. "You're getting so tall, Julian. You look more and more like your father every day."

"So Dad was a good-looking man," Julian said with a laugh.

In a slow, matter-of-fact voice, she replied, "Yes, he was, son. Yes, yes he was."

"I know you've told me that he was hit by a car, Mom, but you've never really mentioned much about it, and you know, I kind of knew that it was painful for you, so I never really brought it up, but I always wanted to find out more. Are you okay to talk about it now? How did it happen? I…you know…just want to know."

"Well, you deserve that much," his mother replied. "Let's get to making dinner and get settled down for a bit, and then maybe we can talk a little more," she said with a hesitant, not-expecting-to-have-this-conversation kind of voice.

Meal preparation was commonly shared by Julian and his mother. Ever since he was a young lad, she had always included him with *this and that* in the kitchen. Tonight, Julian's job was to peel and chop the onions and get the noodles ready to boil on the stove.

While she tended to the ground beef, adding spices in an old black cast-iron pan that she loved to use, she said to Julian, "Now come on. Get the noodles started first. You know they need a long time to boil."

Soon the mushroom soup would be mixed in with the ground beef sautéing in the big black pan. The noodles then spread onto two plates and smothered in the soupy concoction. That was dinner. It was a simple meal. Cheap as it comes but gratefully enjoyed by Julian and his mother as they really never had complaints. They knew that they had each other, and that's all that really mattered. It made every meal delicious.

Toward the end of supper, Julian's mother took a long drink of her lemon water, and placing the glass back down on the table, Julian noticed that her hand was shaking slightly. That's what caused him to look up at her and notice that her eyes were swollen, welled up with tears. He asked, "Are you okay, Mom? What's wrong?"

"I was just thinking about your father, Julian. One thing you should know is that your father died as a hero."

"What do you mean? He was hit by a car you said, right?"

"Yes, he was, son, but what happened was that your father dived out in front of a car to save a little boy's life. A toddler had gotten away from the people who were watching after him, and he ran into the street. They said it didn't take your father a split second to make the decision to dive out and sacrifice his own life to save that little boy. I remember he was around the same age you were. Your father had to have known in that instant that he would never see you grow up but that his sacrifice meant that another little boy would have the chance to."

Julian slumped in his chair and said with a quiver in his voice, "I never knew." He then leaned forward, reached across the table to grab his mother's trembling hands, consoling each other as they momentarily wept.

Then Julian's mother drew back. In an effort to show him strength, she quickly wiped the tears from her eyes and scooped up her dinner plate saying, "I need to get these dishes started. They're not going to wash themselves. And you need to get busy on your home-work. You have such wonderful grades, and we can't let them slip. We all have our duties. Life goes on, and our task is to *carry on*. I know that's what your father would want. He'd want us to carry on. So no more pity parties, young man. You and I both have things to do."

She wiped yet another tear from her eye and made her way over to the sink. Julian, with a heavy heart, also wiped the tears from his eyes, got up from the table, and walked into the living room where he picked up his book on quantum physics and began reading where he had left off.

The day turned into night, and Julian read on until he had finally given into the gravity of sleep. Doting over him as a mother would, she leaned forward and gave him a soft kiss on the top center of his head saying, "Come on, son. It's time to go to bed now."

Like a rag doll on autopilot, the droopy-eyed Julian made his way down the long, narrow hallway toward his room. His mother, behind him, made sure she tucked him into the bed and kissed him once again on the head saying, "You've grown so fast, Julian. These days we share will someday pass. You have great things ahead of you."

And those days did indeed pass and all too quickly as Julian came into his final year of high school. In that time, as always, he could be found sitting on the front porch of his house with a book in one hand and the other subconsciously picking away at the paint that was peeling on the bench where he sat or lying on his stomach in bed, book in hand, bare feet in the air and a night-light to help him read.

There was also a quiet place of refuge near a creek down by the high school. A narrow path led into it. He was one of a very few that knew of it. He would go there for solitude and to take time out for more reading. It brought him comfort and peace.

In school, it seemed he was almost always the first one in each class and then the last one to leave. He always had an extra question or two for the teachers. They thought of him as the mind sponge. In the faculty lounge, they would say, "There's just no limit to how much information you can put in his head."

For Julian, schoolwork was easy. He never had to study much to make straight As, but his passion was math and science. When he wasn't required to read and learn the other subjects, it was always math and science that he pursued. It's what drove him. It was almost an addiction. He also had a powerful imagination and loved music. Often when something moved him, his brain would play a song that would match the moment of whatever he was experiencing.

Julian was considered a good-looking young man by most of the girls that went to his high school. His body was athletic and toned, slender, as he played basketball throughout middle school and high school. With wavy brown hair, he had the soft round eyes of his mother but brown like his father. His eyebrows were full and defined. He was a cross between Rob Lowe and Tom Brady. He got along with everyone except one in particular, a disgruntled sort named Ed Hanson. His full name was Edward Hanson Jr. His father was known as Eddie. Ed was leary of everyone, suspicious no one really meant what they said. He was sure that everyone was a fake and that Julian was the biggest fraud of them all! Ed was a tortured soul. His father was a joke around town with a long arrest record of petty crimes and public drunkenness. Behind closed doors, he would beat his wife and justified it to Ed by saying, "If you don't keep a woman in line, they will run all over you," and that his mother got what she deserved. Ed believed the things that he learned from his father but hated him just the same. That's why Ed Jr. never wanted to be known as Eddie and Ed hated it when anyone called him Eddie. He was Ed! And Ed had a high IQ but cared little about school, thinking of it as a requirement of the *system*. He kept his grades low because in the twisted workings of his mind, he felt that if he was underestimated, he would have the upper hand. Ed was skinny and taller than most. He had lots of freckles and dark-brown hair that he kept short by cutting it himself. His nose and mouth were narrow. His ears were small but stuck out from his head. His dark-brown eyes always seemed to be calculating his surroundings. Everyone gave him a wide berth except for Julian. He felt it better to stand in the face of a bully, and he did so the day they clashed. That happened when Julian showed up to basketball practice early on a Friday before game day to work on some free throws when he heard a low-tone, angry voice from the other side of the retracted bleachers. As he creeped his way around to investigate, he saw Ed holding the front collar of a scared freshman kid and then slapped his face with the other. Julian shouted, "Back off, man. Let him go!"

"What? Are you protecting your little girlfriend?"

"I said let him go!"

"What are you going to do about it?" Julian then hurled the basketball he was holding at him, and Ed let go to side step the ball coming straight at his head. The ninth grader ran off to get help. Ed gave Julian a cold look and said, "You think you're some kind of hero like your dead father?"

"Better to have a dead father than your father, EDDIE! You, loser!" And with that, it was on! Ed charged at Julian, but Julian didn't back away. They traded blows even as the coach and janitor ran toward them yelling to stop.

As they were pulled apart, Ed kept shouting, "This isn't over. This isn't over!"

Julian fired back, "Really, Eddie? Not over, Eddie? Eddie, Eddie, Eddie, not over? I was hoping we could be friends, Eddie!"

"Enough, you two!" the basketball coach Hal Snellgose shouted. Then he looked at the janitor who had a firm grasp on Ed and said, "Take him to the principal's office." Then turning to deal with Julian, he released him saying, "What the hell, son? Control yourself!"

"Coach, he was slapping around that Seacord kid. I had to do something."

The coach had a fact-of-life stare on his face as he bowed forward slightly and struck the back of his right hand against the palm of his left saying, "Not that, Julian, of course you had to step in. It's the taunting I'm talking about! You're above that, son, really? With the Eddie, Eddie, Eddie crap, really?"

Julian was red faced and trying to control his nerves as his heart rate was high. He began measuring his intake of breath to help regulate his heartbeat and said, "You're right, coach, but he's just such a...a dick. He's bad to everyone!"

Coach Hal now but again slapping the back of his hand against his palm, slower and more rhythmic with each word, he said, "It matters not what another man is but rather what sort of man you choose to be!"

Julian, still trying to slow his breath, said, "You're right, coach. I'm sorry... I am...but he's a bad seed."

"Do you think making him more angry is going to somehow make him good? Look at me, do you?"

"No," Julian said.

"Well, son, do you think you're only going to run into one bad seed your whole life?" Julian just sulked as Coach Hal continued, "You're going to have to be tolerant of people because you don't know their background or what makes them the way they are! Stand up to bullies, yes, but don't sink to their level, son!" Julian's face was still flush though his breathing had slowed.

"I know, I know, you're right, coach. You're right! I just lost it!"

"It's all right, Julian, but just remember, sometimes a bad seed just needs a good example, so be one!" For Julian, Coach Hal was a father figure, and he learned a deeper level of patience for the misguided. But Julian was always learning. His mind was ever expanding, and he was growing smarter by the day. Girlfriends were few and far between though, as he rarely recognized when he was being flirted with. His mind was so frequently submerged in profundities that he would often find himself alone and engulfed in the mysteries of the universe. He could see mathematics in everything scientific and science in everything mathematic. He was rapidly making connections between them both. It was for him as though the two were merging as one. It wasn't ambition that fueled his quest. It was the natural yearning of his mind, the restless, unbridled genius within him that was always pushing him forward.

And it all paid off with a letter that came just two and a half weeks before his graduation, a letter that would bring his mother her greatest joy and her second greatest sorrow.

* * * * *

She was sitting in the living room enjoying a rare moment of quiet in the old leather chair where Julian had often fell asleep reading books when she was suddenly startled by the slamming of the front door as Julian charged through with an open letter in his hand. He shouted, "Mama! Mama! I got it! You're not going to believe it!" he yelled as he waved the letter in the air. "I got accepted into MIT! I got accepted! I got accepted into MIT, Mama, and they're giving me a full-ride scholarship!"

She sprung from her seat to greet his excitement, hugging him and saying, "I knew it, son. I knew it. I knew that you could do it." With her hands grasping the outside of his shoulders, she stepped back slightly saying, "Julian, you're going to make people's dreams come true someday. You've got something in you. Lord, I don't know where it comes from, but you've sure got it, and I know that you're going to do well with it."

"Thanks, Mom," he said with a chuckle. "No pressure, right?"

For Julian and his mother, that summer would seem to go by faster than any other. On a rainy night in late August, Julian and his mother would find themselves at the local bus station, Julian's hair still dripping and matted from the pelting rain that drenched him on the way from the parking lot to the door. His mother's hair was covered with one of those old plastic rain bonnets. As she removed it from her head, she looked at Julian and then at the floor and then back at Julian.

Julian, sitting straightforward looking at the walls that were badly in need of a fresh coat of paint, looked down at the ground too and then back up at the plain walls. He turned his head to look at his mother to find her looking at him. He could tell that she wanted to say something, just anything, but everything had already been said. Nothing left now but the heartbreak of separation.

He looked at her and said, "It's okay, Mama. I'm going to be back, you know. I'm not going away forever."

"I know, son, but I'm going to worry about you."

"I'm going to worry about you too, Mama. You're going to be all alone."

"I don't want you to worry about me," she said. "I don't want you to think about what I'm doing or if I'm lonely or not. You need to do what you need to do. Study hard and be a good boy, and I'll be all right."

"Oh, for crying out loud, Mama," he said. "Of course, I'm going to worry about you. Just two weeks ago, there was that murder not more than ten or twelve miles from the house!"

With a look of confident disregard, Julian's mother said, "Murder happens everywhere. I'll be just fine, and so will you. Oh, and you know what I heard about that murder? They brought in that Hansen kid for questioning."

"No, really? Ed Hansen?"

"Yep, Ed Junior."

"Great, so much for not worrying."

Just then, the sudden clank of the departure bell and a voice that sounded like a hot-dog vendor at a baseball game came over the PA and said, "Boarding, now boarding for route 337, boarding for route 337, west gate."

"Well, that's me, Mama," Julian said as he stood up, grasping his luggage in one hand and hiking his backpack over his shoulder. "You can call me anytime during the trip. It's going to be a long, lonely bus ride, you know?"

She stood up, leaned forward, and gave him a firm hug. He was barely able to return the hug, hampered by all of his belongings. She said, "You know, don't be surprised if I talk to you the whole way."

He gave his mother one last quick kiss on the cheek as he scampered toward the exit gate with a handful of other riders who had the same route. He turned and yelled back, "My cell phone is fully charged!"

His destination on this bus ride was Chicago where he would then transfer to a connecting bus that would take him the rest of the way to Massachusetts. His travels would end there, but his journey would just begin.

* * * * *

Julian's mother kept in contact with him periodically throughout his trip until it came time to sleep. The bus arrived at the station about twenty minutes ahead of schedule. Julian was fast asleep in his seat when the bus driver nudged him on the shoulder and said, "Come on, sleepyhead, can't stay on this bus. I've got another trip right back to Chicago."

Julian sat up and leaned forward, rubbing his eyes to get the sleep out. He looked around the bus, grabbed his belongings, and exited in a dreary kind of slow stagger, still waiting to fully wake up.

This bus station was much different from the one that he left in his small town. It was, full of people going here and going there, other new students arriving as well. But fortunately that meant that with all of that activity, there would be plenty of taxicabs waiting outside as MIT was only about five miles away.

Julian hailed the first open taxi that he saw as it pulled sharply up to the curb. He popped open the door and threw in his luggage saying to the taxicab driver, "Could you ta—," and the cabby quickly cut him off.

"Let me guess, you need a ride to MIT."

Julian said, "Yep. I take it that was an easy guess."

The taxi driver just smirked and said, "I've been working this job for quite a while, and I damn sure know what time of the year it is. I'll have you there shortly. It's about a fifteen-dollar ride, tip included."

With the glow of morning light still in the air, Julian arrived on campus. Leaning toward the front seat, he handed over the fifteen dollars and thanked him for the ride.

Julian surveyed the near-chaotic scene of new students, all exploring the campus and searching for their dorms. The excitement was contagious. Julian took in the sight of the dorm buildings and was in awe. Some of them looked like square blocks etched out in the appearance of a giant microchip. His dorm-room building was one of two that were indeed breathtaking, Art Decoish in style and seeming to lean in on one another in a balanced acrobat of artwork and architecture combined, not just designed to house students but also meant to inspire the mind.

Outside, hundreds of students were hustling and bustling in all directions, carrying everything they needed from lounge chairs to blenders to books, all aiming for their destinations, while others were playing Frisbee, some playing football. Others had already settled in and had pulled out small grills for burgers and hot dogs, even flat irons for making eggs and pancakes.

Julian made his way through the large double doors. Just inside the main hallway posted on the walls was a long list bearing the names and room numbers of the students. Julian scanned the list, looking for his name as a slender, beautiful student walked up next to him. She was simply dressed in a short-sleeved shirt and capri jeans, the girl-next-door kind of look. Her long dark hair was gathered into a high bouncy pony-tail. She finished a conversation she was having with another new arrival and began looking for her name on the list as well. She and Julian turned together and bumped into each other face-to-face.

Julian, in an awkward moment, took in her beauty, paused, and said, "I'm so sorry. I didn't see you standing there."

She said, "It's okay. I didn't see you either."

"I'm Julian," he said as he changed his backpack to his left so he could shake hands with her.

She shook his hand firmly and said, "My name is Rebecca."

"Nice to meet you, Rebecca. Can I call you Becky?"

"No," she replied with a smile. "I left that name behind when I grew up. I prefer Rebecca. But can I call you Jules?"

"No," he said with a slight grin. "I see what you mean, that doesn't really work for me either. Let's just go with Julian... Rebecca!"

"Deal," she said, then continued, "Well, this sure is a busy day for all of us. Maybe I'll see you around campus," she said as she turned back to find her name on the wall.

"Maybe so," Julian said hopefully as he walked away slowly, still watching her search the list. This time was different. He took a long, hard look at this young woman, and there was something about her that shined for him. Julian took a deep breath and said to himself in a low voice, "Now there is something special right there. Yes, indeed."

He spun back around and went back to the task of finding his room. He went up the spiral stairs to the third floor, and once there, he made his way down the wide hallway that seemed awfully narrow with the mass of students all finding their way. He reached his new home, room 337, and thought, "Huh. That's a familiar number. Maybe I should play it in the lottery."

He pushed the door open to find a wiry-haired young man sitting atop his luggage with his back slumped against the wall. He looked up at Julian and said, "I guess you're my roomie, huh?"

"I guess you would be the same," Julian replied. "Nice to meet you. My name is Julian, Julian Phillips."

"Of course, it's nice to meet me, Julian, Julian Phillips. My name's Drake Wallace, and I'm having a rough day."

"Yeah, you look a little disheveled. What's up with you?"

"Well, it's day two on campus for me. Last night I got here early and decided to go have a few. I guess I had a few too many, and I'm a bit of a mess right now. My head is killing me. You got anything for pain?"

"I think I've got aspirin somewhere," Julian said. Drake looked disappointed.

Looking upward, Drake said, "Lord, help me through this one, and I swear I'll get through the next one all by myself." Julian noted there were no words of self-improvement in his mockery of a prayer.

Then with a look of curiosity on his face, Julian said, "Hey, I'm a Phillips, and you're a Wallace. Don't they normally pair people by alphabet?"

Drake said, "Yeah, they do with the leftovers, but most of the time, they pair people according to grade-point average, area of study, and even geographic location, your origin."

"Oh, then you're either pretty smart, or we lived close to each other."

Drake replied, "Well, I graduated with a 5.64 counting college credits. How about you?"

"I graduated with a 5.61. So that leaves us pretty close on GPA. I come from Beech Grove, Indiana. Whereabouts are you from?"

"Ha, see! They got us on two counts. I'm from southeast Indianapolis, just a three iron and a pitching wedge away from your neck of the woods."

"Golfer, are you?"

"No. Duffer is more like it. But it's a drinking sport. So that and bowling are pretty all right by me."

"Drinking sport?" Julian asked. "I've never seen any member of the PGA with a drink in their hand other than an Arnold Palmer."

"Well," Drake replied, "you don't see pro bowlers with a cocktail in their hand either. See, the fact of the matter is that golf was invented by the Irish. They're known to have a drink or two, and the average bottle of whiskey carries eighteen shots. You ever wonder why there's eighteen holes in golf?"

"Not really, but it does seem odd that it's not ten, fifteen, or twenty."

"Well, as the story goes, if you did one shot after each hole, by the time you were done with a full round, you were also done with a full bottle."

"I'll have to take your word for it, but it sounds like a great way to get a DUI in a golf cart! Anyway, I guess we're going to have to figure out whose bed is whose," as he looked at both beds on either side of the room.

"Doesn't matter to me. I'll probably pass out in the wrong bed from time to time anyway so…"

"Great," Julian said with a touch of disappointment in his voice. "I guess I'll have to figure out how to get along with you, but you're lucky. I'm pretty easygoing!" Thinking to himself, *I hear you Coach Hal, bad seed, good example! I know the drill.*

Drake said, "I, myself, am pretty good at going easy, so yin and yang here. We'll probably work out all right."

Julian took a breath, looked around, and said, "Well, I guess I'll take the bed on the right here, seeing as how my luggage is three feet closer to it than the other bed."

"Sounds like good logic to me. Hey, you know what? Why don't you just unpack your stuff real quick and then come with me down to the pub where I made my grand entrance yesterday. I need a little hair of the dog, if you know what I mean."

"Well, I can join you, I suppose, but I don't drink really. And how is it that you do? You're not old enough, and neither am I."

"You don't drink?" Drake said. "Get a fake ID. Works for me."

"Hmm…not going to do that, and no, I've never actually drank alcohol in my life."

"Who's never drank alcohol in their life?" Drake said with an exclamation point in his voice.

"Well, by my count, so far it's just me, Donald Trump, Dr. Phil, and Steve Jobs."

"Well, you're going to be a lot of fun," Drake said. "And what good did not drinking do those guys?"

"Well, one is worth millions and millions and the other two made billions…so?"

"Yeah, well, Jobs never drank, never smoked, and died of cancer just the same."

"Well, the list of alcoholics that made it to an early grave is pretty extensive."

"That may be so, Julian. But one thing you've got to realize is not everybody wants to live a long life. Not everybody deserves to either. So if my choices are to give up the things that I like, give up the food that I want to eat and the things that I want to drink so that a boring-ass life like that can go on for an extra ten or fifteen years, no thanks. I'd rather fill an *early grave*. I'd rather laugh with the sinners than cry with the saints, pal. Besides, George Burns used to drink, and he smoked fifteen to twenty cigars a day, and he lived to be over a hundred."

"Well," Julian said, "when it all boils down, then I guess life is just a roll of the dice. Besides, it's not like I don't drink because I'm disciplined or anything like that. I just never thought about it much."

"I think about it all the time, but I'll have to work on you. I'll get you to have a drink with me at some point or another."

"Well, as far as having a drink with you, ya never know what the future holds. It's food for thought. Right now I need food for my belly. That pub over there, do they serve breakfast?"

"Well, yeah, they serve breakfast if your idea of breakfast is a cheeseburger. That grill is open twenty-four hours a day, but I don't think they sling eggs. I'm sure we'll find common ground somewhere, you and I, but for now, your breakfast is a cheeseburger, and mine is a Bloody Mary."

* * * *

Julian spent most of his time doing the same things that he did in high school. He could always be found outside on the steps of the dorm reading a book or in his bunk doing the same. He could be found studying in the library, poring through information, always looking for more to study, more to understand.

By all accounts, Drake was more brilliant than Julian. But Julian's mind always shined brighter because Drake's time was spent in pursuit of whatever pleased him at the moment, which also changed by the moment. Drake was handsome, sharp-witted, and charismatic. His wiry hair was jet-black. He had piercing blue eyes and a Mathew McConaughey smile. While Julian was handsome in his own right, Drake, on the other hand, could've been a model. Women were drawn to him much the way a moth is drawn to a flame. But Drake wasn't interested in romance. He would move from one conquest to another. It was more about feeding his ego.

But Julian's eye was drawn to only one… Rebecca. He would see her there in the laundry or in the cafeteria, in the hallways occasionally between classes, always the long look, now and then a brief conversation. For Julian, she seemed to have a glow around her. He always loved the way her nose would crinkle slightly when she would smile or the way her eyes would light up upon excitement or discovery. She had perfect, full, pouty lips, and they were adorably decorated by two dimples on either side. She never dressed sexy or fancy, and that made her all the more appealing to him.

Though there were plenty of offers, she, like Julian, didn't date very much. She was focused on her work, and although, like most of the women on campus, she found Drake to be charismatic and handsome, she, on the other hand, never accepted his advances. She was attracted to substance rather than flare, and she, too, had eyes for only one... Julian.

* * * * *

As time wore on, so did the patience of Drake's professors. At one time or another, it seemed that all of them had scolded Drake for his laziness, for neglecting his brilliance and not taking advantage of his mind's potential.

Though Drake and Julian had by now become very good friends, Drake's jealousy of Julian had grown because by contrast, Julian was constantly praised for his accomplishments. His professors were always amazed with Julian's brilliance, his ideas, and his drive. They were quite the opposite, Julian and Drake, but friends nonetheless.

On one particular day, sitting in the school cafeteria, Julian proposed the concept of artificially creating a wormhole. Drake disputed that the idea was even possible. Julian continued to explain while Drake pulled a french fry from his tray and flung it toward the cafeteria line at a group of freshman, striking one of them in the forehead. The boy spun around, not sure from which direction the french fry had come from. Drake snickered, holding his head down. "Did you see that? Got him right in the forehead! Did you see that?"

"Yeah, I saw it. But what I failed to see was the point. Drake, I just don't understand you sometimes."

"Come on, I'm just having a little fun. Let your hair down once in a while, Julian. Why are you always so uptight? That was funny!"

And just then, Rebecca walked by the table where Julian and Drake were seated, accompanied by one of her group-study partners, a cute little blonde. "Hi, Julian, how are you?"

Julian smiled. "Just fine, always good to see you." Rebecca returned the smile warmly but only gave a cursory nod toward Drake as she and her friend found a table for themselves.

Drake looked at Julian and said, "Wow, she gave you a look. What was that about?"

Julian said, "I don't know, but I'll probably ask her out one of these days."

"Well, what's taking you so long, my man? That's a mighty fine target."

"I never thought of her as a target," Julian replied. "But she is mighty fine."

"Don't wait too long," Drake continued. "She's bound to give me a yes sooner or later."

"What do you mean?"

"Well, actually, I have asked her out a few times, but she keeps turning me down."

"Then why don't you go after that cute little blonde?"

"Because I've already drank from that fountain."

"So what makes Rebecca so special?" Julian asked.

"Well, it's always the one you can't have that is the most valued prize, so go make a move, old buddy. Ask her out. I doubt you'll make out any better than I did."

"What do you mean by that?"

"Well, I'm a pretty prime piece of real estate, and if she can't recognize that, I don't see how you're going to get anywhere with her either, although she did seem interested." Drake, attempting to project failure, continued saying, "But in a kind of *whatever* sort of way."

"I'm a pretty nice piece of real estate myself, Drake. And maybe she just doesn't want a guy that's full of himself."

"Ow, that's going to leave a mark," Drake said as he stretched out his legs and leaned back with both hands behind the back of his head. He continued, "Yeah, well, I'm pretty impressed with me. I have to say that."

Julian looked straight up, rolling his eyes and shaking his head. He turned back toward Drake. "You are a piece of work, my friend," he said with a chuckle. "A real piece of work."

Julian glanced over to the table where Rebecca and her friend were sitting. They both looked simultaneously in Julian's direction, and Rebecca covered her nose and mouth and gave a little laugh as she quickly looked back toward her friend, making it obvious that Julian was the subject of their conversation. Julian looked at Drake and said, "Did you see that?"

"Sure," he said in a mocking tone, "but what I failed to see was the point."

Julian laughed saying, "Yeah, well, maybe I should have flung a french fry at her instead."

"Touché." Drake sat up, folded his arms in front of him, and held his head back slightly with a cocky flair. He gave a nod in Rebecca's direction and said, "Let's see how far that quick wit of yours gets you with her."

Julian jumped up holding his chin sharply and struck a pose reminiscent of a matador. He clapped his hands once and said, "No time like the present! Seize the day! E pluribus unum!" as he moved in the direction of Rebecca and out of Drake's hearing range.

Drake watched with interest as Julian first addressed Rebecca, then acknowledged her friend, and then turned back to Rebecca. He watched as she stared at Julian with a glowing smile on her face. As Julian continued talking to her, Rebecca's smile widened, and when Julian paused, Drake watched her head nod up and down, and though he couldn't read her lips per se, it wasn't hard to tell what her response was. Julian said something more, nodded to her friend, and gave a wave as he walked away from the table.

Julian casually walked by the table where Drake was still sitting. He leaned in and said, "Meeting her at the rec hall at six thirty, so move over, Casanova."

Julian faded into the crowd toward the exit while Drake sat with a defeated look on his face. He waved his hand in the air mockingly and said to himself, "Seize the spew, close cover before striking, remove card quickly, e pluribus buffoonum…what the hell was that?"

* * * * *

Julian decided to arrive at the rec hall a half hour early, if for no other reason than to have a chance to stave off nervous anticipation. Rather than dressing to impress, Julian thought it best to dress casual and comfortable. That's the way she had always seen him, and she had always seemed to like what she saw, so why take a chance on changing that now? He wore his slightly scuffed white Adidas sneakers, his favorite pair of jeans with holes cut out on the knees, Billy Squier-style, and a blue and gold T-shirt that said "Indiana Pacers." As he approached the entrance to the hall, he noticed the sliding glass doors were open to let in the fresh spring air. As he entered, three students were just exiting, two boys with a girl walking between them, the boys trying to talk over each other in an obvious attempt to win her affection. She, however, looked more like they were giving her a headache.

He looked to his left and saw two pool tables with games in session. There was a vacant ping-pong table and next to that, three video games occupied by two players. On his right, he saw a cluster of tables and chairs and a snack-bar area where he immediately spotted Rebecca's smiling face looking straight at him. In that instant, for him, the rest of the room disappeared. He turned and walked straight toward her as though he were being pulled by a vortex that only he could see.

She stood to greet him with a beaming smile as he approached. She took his breath away in her simple sleeveless summer dress that was speckled with white-and-purple flowers. He looked down at her, cocked his head slightly, and he said, "Looks like we're both early."

"Yeah, I guess I wanted to get here early just to relax. Guess I'm a little nervous."

"Same here," he said. "I'm not sure why. I feel like I'm in high school."

She giggled and said, "Well, what now?"

"I was hoping you'd be in the mood for a walk. There's a stream not too far from here and a little area where I go to read now and then. I thought it might be a nice quiet place to talk, or if you would prefer dancing in a crowded bar where we can barely hear each other, I can make that happen too."

"No," she said, "a quiet area by the stream sounds pretty sweet to me."

There was still plenty of daylight as they strolled along, but the brightest part of the day was long gone. He looked at her and said, "Would you think it was old-fashioned if I asked, 'May I hold your hand as we walk, my dear?'"

She laughed and said, "Yes, it would, but I like old-fashioned. I'd like that."

He took her hand and asked, "Are you hungry?"

"A little. I'm not starving though."

He said, "I know a great little place not too far from here. But let's have just a quick stop by the stream first. There's something I want to show you."

In her best, playful Southern-belle accent, she said, "Something down by the river you want to show me? I do declare this is our first date. But I suppose I can trust a gentleman like you."

In his own best Southern accent, he replied, "Why yes, ma'am, you can certainly trust me. I'm as harmless as they come." She gave him a smile and squeezed his hand. They talked as they strolled down the sidewalk which eventually led to a well-worn path that wound through a wide-open field. About four minutes into the walk down the sandy path, Julian paused and pointed about fifty yards away to a small cluster of elm trees. "Here, it's right over here."

As they approached the elm trees, Julian gestured, reaching out with his hand as though he was opening a door, and said, "Allow me." He pulled back a few branches that revealed a small opening, and holding back the branches, he bowed and said, "After you, my dear."

She returned to her Southern-belle accent and replied, "Why, you are a gentleman indeed," and she ducked through the branches. It seemed to be leading her to the left, so she asked, "Am I going in the right direction?"

Julian came up behind her, put his hands over her eyes, and said, "Let me lead you these last few steps."

"You can lead me. Just don't lead me on."

"Never," he said. "I want you to stand right here for just a moment. I'm going to take my hands off of your eyes, but I want you to keep them closed for just a second. I've got something I have to do."

"Well, okay," she said with nervous anticipation. "But can I at least take a peek?"

"No," he said as he scurried to light half-dozen candles that he had suspended from the trees and dangling from the branches in a wide circle. He lit the last candle and said, "Okay, I'm ready. Open your eyes."

When she did, she gasped, put her hands over her nose and mouth, and said, "Oh my God! This is so cool." There was a beautiful clearing among the trees with a wide-open view of the stream that flowed by. The tree branches created a natural canopy, and under which was a surreal glow from the candles that cast light on the centerpiece of a rustic butcher-block table with no legs. In the center of the table, there was one large, round, short candle and a bottle of wine with two stemmed glasses. Napkins held silverware rolled inside. There was plush green grass that covered the entire open area, and on either side of the table were folded white blankets to be used as makeshift pillows. On the ground at the far end of the butcher-block table was a twenty-gallon blue-and-white Coleman cooler, and on top of that sat a hibachi propane grill.

Julian walked over to Rebecca, extended his elbow, and said, "May I escort you to your table, ma'am?"

She replied with a smile, "Why yes, that would be lovely."

Julian had all of the ingredients prepped ahead of time for steak au poivre, kabob vegetables, and new potatoes. They chatted and made small talk as he prepared their meals. Day gave way into night as the candlelight shimmered on the leaves and branches above, creating a magical, sparkling effect. Rebecca gazed at the beauty overhead, and then she looked at Julian. "Thank you for all of this. It is amazing and makes me feel so special. I don't accept offers to go out on dates very often. I'm kind of picky."

"Well, I'm glad I made the cut. My roommate said he didn't fare so well."

"Drake?" she replied sharply. "I wouldn't go out with him to save my life. I mean, he's smart and good-looking and all, but he's a human train wreck. Besides that, he's just a player. Do you remember Susan, the girl I was having lunch with earlier?"

"Yeah, the blond girl."

"Yeah, her, well, he charmed her pants off until he got what he wanted, and then he moved on as though nothing had ever happened. She was really hurt by that. Some girls might be fine with one-night stands, but Susan is not one of them. She didn't respond to his advances at first, but the more she turned him down, the more he persisted. Then once he got what he wanted, poof, he was gone."

Julian said, "Believe me, I know what you mean. I'm his roommate, and I was thinking about having a revolving door installed in our dorm room. Don't get me wrong. I like the guy and all, and I consider him a friend, but he doesn't think about the future much. He pretty much just lives for the day."

"Some of my girlfriends and I refer to him as *the beautiful mess*. But enough about him," she said. "I don't want to waste the ambiance. I'd rather focus on you."

"I was thinking the same thing about you," he said as he leaned in and gave her a soft, gentle kiss. They paused for a moment, looked at each other, and smiled. The first kiss led to a second, a third, and a fourth, each lasting a bit longer than the one before.

That first date would also lead to a second, a third, and a fourth, also lasting a bit longer than the one before. Julian always walked Rebecca back to her dorm room. Sometimes he would stay the night, but on the times that he didn't, he would always make sure she locked her door, insisting that she do so.

"I'm glad I have you to help me feel safe," she said one night. "You know, they never did find out who killed Janet Barnes."

Julian said, "I remember that. That was about two years ago. She was a senior, wasn't she?"

"Yeah. She was just about to graduate too, had her whole life ahead of her."

"Her parents must have been devastated."

Rebecca replied, "More than that, she was an only child. It crushed them."

"That's just so sad. All the more reason I worry about you."

"Don't worry about me, Julian. Murders happen everywhere. I'll be fine."

Julian paused and said, "And so will I."

Rebecca looked at him questioningly. "What?"

"Never mind, you just reminded me of something my mother said a few years back. Well, anyway, I've got to get going. I've got exams in the morning, and I think you do too."

They both leaned in for a kiss good night and smiled at each other. Rebecca went inside and closed the door. Julian would always wait until he heard the sound of the dead-bolt lock before going on his way.

Julian and Rebecca quickly became an official item. They spent all of their free time together. Rebecca excelled academically, but none shined brighter than Julian. He was constantly receiving campus-wide accolades for one achievement or another. And while Drake excelled academically as well, he grew weary of being badgered by his professors who always insisted that he was capable of so much more if he just applied himself. Drake's resentment of Julian silently grew.

One stormy night toward the close of Julian and Drake's senior year, Julian made his way back to his dorm room to discover it slightly open with music playing somewhat loudly coming from within. It was the song "Riders on the Storm" by the Doors. He pushed the door open slightly to discover the room dark, the only light coming from the street lamps outside and the lightning in the night sky.

As Julian pushed the door open farther, he could see the darkened silhouette of Drake sitting naked, Indian-style, on the floor facing the windows watching the lightning on display. As the light flickered, Julian could see a bottle of Fireball at Drake's side. Julian stood in the doorway, pondering the moment and thinking to himself, *There is never a dull moment with this guy*, and then said, "Okay, Drake, what's going on?"

There was no reply. Julian rolled his backpack off his shoulder and set it by the door. He moved to his bed and sat, noticing there was a single lit candle sitting on the floor in front of Drake. He said hesitantly, "Hello?" Still no reply. After a few seconds, Julian said more forcefully, "Drake, are you on something?"

After a few seconds, Drake replied in a sort of loud whisper, "Yes, I am."

Julian asked, "What are you on?"

Drake answered, "The floor."

Just then, "Riders on the Storm" ended, and just as quickly, it began again. Drake had the song on a loop. Julian said, "Good song choice, Drake. It matches the weather," just as lightning lit up the sky and the thunder crashed and rumbled.

He continued to stare straight forward, never changing from the sitting position that he was in when Julian first entered the room. Drake finally said, "Do you believe in God?"

Julian replied, "Well, yeah. Yeah, I do."

Drake continued, "Do you believe that some people are evil?"

"Well, yeah, of course, that goes without saying. If there's good, there's evil."

"Then some people belong in hell? Drake asked.

"Yeah, of course."

"Do you believe that Hitler belongs in hell?"

"Well, I'm not supposed to judge, I suppose, but it seems like a no-brainer that that's where Hitler would be."

"Do you think he was born evil?"

Julian responded, "I don't think anyone is born evil, but over time, if they chose to, they become evil."

Then Drake said, "So if Hitler died when he was a baby, he'd probably be in heaven right now?"

"I never thought of it that way, but I guess you'd be right." Then after pausing for a moment, Julian said, "This is pretty deep, and it's also getting pretty late. Maybe it's time to move into shallower waters and put these thoughts to bed. Let them rest overnight."

"All good and well," Drake said as he reached over and grabbed his pint of Fireball. He pursed his lips, chugged down a shot, and said, "I'll be going to bed soon. But let me ask you something, Julian. Have you ever really listened to The Doors?"

Julian said, "Yeah, I have. It's all great stuff."

"No," Drake replied sharply. "No." And then his tone became groggy again. "Have you ever really listened?"

"Okay, yeah. You sound a little spooky now. But yes, I have."

"Not just this song, but there's a piece that Jim Morrison did. It's called 'American Prayer.' Have you ever heard of it?"

"No, I've never heard of it. No."

"It's not a song," he said, taking another swig. "It's just Morrison rambling on about life and his view of the world. You have to listen to it."

"Why do I have to listen to it? Why is it so important?"

"There was a part in it where Morrison said when he was just a young boy, he came across a traffic accident that had a bunch of American Indians on the way to farm fields to work. It was on a remote highway. The accident had just happened. There was no help to be found anywhere, and there were bodies strewn all over the road, some dead, others dying. These Indians, they believed that if they died suddenly and violently that their spirit would move to another body. Morrison swore that one, maybe two of them, had entered his mind, into his soul, and that's where they remained. Maybe his mind was altered at that time, making perception difficult, making reality hard to interpret. But we're not that different he and I… I feel a connection with him."

"What's the connection to you? Julian asked. "I mean, how does Jim Morrison relate to you?"

"I don't know. I don't know, but it feels like I'm not supposed to be here. I know it sounds crazy, but it has been this way my whole life, long before I ever heard 'American Prayer.' It feels like I was a mistake that somehow fell through the cracks."

"Well then, if you feel that way, then make the best of your life that you can."

"Oh, I do, Julian. I'm having a rip-roaring time. I can tell you that!"

"I'm sure you are, but I meant by helping people, by making a positive impact on the world."

"Ha!" Drake said maniacally. "People need to solve their own problems."

Julian tried to reason with him sympathetically saying, "We're all human, and we all make mistakes, so what about at least helping the people that we've hurt along the way?"

"If I've hurt anyone, then that would be their problem to deal with because I don't always know when someone's going to hurt me or even when I might hurt someone else, so it's on them to fix it or feel better or whatever."

"Are you saying that you're not responsible for the choices that you make?"

Drake paused and then said, "No, but there are times when I feel like I'm just a puppet on a string, and I don't know who the puppet master is. But he keeps me dancing this little dance."

Julian thought that at this point, he was listening to the distorted ramblings of a drunken madman.

With trepidation, Julian offered his hand to Drake to help him stand. Drake grabbed his bottle of Fireball and let Julian help him up. "Let's get you to your bunk." They made their way over for the few steps that it took, and he put the bottle of Fireball into Julian's hand and said, "Take care of this for me, would you? And have a drink!"

"I'm good," Julian said.

"Yeah, you are. You're too good," he said sarcastically as he plopped down on the bed face first. Julian slung his blanket over him. And before Drake drifted off into dreamland, he mumbled, "Listen to 'American Prayer.'"

"I will sometime."

Drake said again, "Listen to it."

It only took a few seconds for Drake to be out cold, and when he was, Julian said, "Good night, beautiful mess."

Chapter 2

The Growing Divide

As time moved on, so would Julian and Drake. Julian graduated at the top of his class and accepted a job with NASA, and he and Rebecca married shortly after graduation. While Drake graduated respectably, he had not taken advantage of his talents, and his academic achievements seemed more like failures.

Julian spent most of his first year with NASA based in Houston, but because he quickly excelled in the areas of science and physics, he became invaluable to NASA, and they began dividing his time between Houston; Washington, D.C. Cape Canaveral; and Silicon Valley.

Drake, on the other hand, had a number of promising career opportunities, but because of his inability to show up on time and a poor work ethic in general, he would lose them all one at a time, moving from one city to the next, making his way around the country.

During this time, Julian and Drake still maintained contact with each other with the odd phone call or the chance meeting in one city or another. They would catch up over lunch or dinner, and Drake would always explain to Julian how impossible the working conditions were at the last place he'd been fired from. On one of these occasions, Julian had a four-hour layover in Atlanta, and Drake was visiting friends in nearby Kennesaw. Drake said that he could make his way down as it was only about a forty-five-minute drive.

Julian was in the mood for a nice steak and wanted to meet at Ruth's Chris. Drake, on the other hand, had another idea. He wanted to meet up at the Cheetah Club. They split the difference and ended up having dinner at Hooters. Julian waited on the sidewalk just outside of terminal B as Drake pulled up in a rented Hummer H2, close to the approximated time that was agreed upon. Drake honked the horn and rolled up alongside the curb and stopped. Julian popped open the back door and slung his brown leather carry-on luggage into the back. He jumped into the front seat and said, "Onward, James! To our place of feasting!"

"Okay. But who the hell is James?"

"James, William, Belvedere, whatever name works for you as my driver. Onward!"

"Was the cabin pressure a little too low or something? Do we need to get you into a decompression chamber?" Drake said as he pulled away from the curb.

"You might be onto something there. I think starvation has got me feeling a little punchy. All they gave me on that plane was a bag of nuts."

"Well, if it's urgent, then I just have to step on it." Drake punched the gas, clipped a couple of orange traffic cones, and headed toward the exit ramp.

Shortly thereafter, they arrived at Hooters and settled into a corner table that had a clear view of the restaurant. The waitress approached with menus in hand. She was a tall, slender blonde with green eyes. She introduced herself as Sally Sue as she handed them the menus. She had a sweet Georgia accent and said, "I'll be taking care of you boys today. What can I start you off with?"

Drake said, "I won't be needing this," as he plopped the menu down on the table. "I'll have a pitcher of light beer and ten of the hottest wings you've got."

She smiled and said, "A man that knows what he wants, how refreshing. And what can I get for you?" she asked Julian.

"Well, I saw on the marquee outside that you've got a snow crab special today. I'll have that and an iced tea so I won't need my menu either." As he plopped it on top of Drake's.

She said, "Wow, fastest order I've taken all week. I'll be right back, fellas."

As she walked away, Drake said, "How does a woman that tall have a butt that small?"

"You know, Drake, it seems like the more things change, the more you don't. But you're right. She does look mighty tasty. So what brought you to Kennesaw?"

"Well, I was visiting some friends of mine, Rodney and Andrea. But that's kind of a sidebar. The main reason is to look into a job with Anderson Technologies."

"Anderson? Weren't you with the Pall Corporation?"

"Yeah, I was. I'm not with them anymore."

"What happened?"

"Well, that's a long story, Julian, but let's just say some people are really hard to work with."

"What do you mean? You said that about the last job you lost."

"How do you know it was my fault?"

"Okay, fair enough. What happened?" Julian asked.

"Well, they put me on a project, all right? And the results that they needed from me had to coincide with the reports that were coming from the science department. Well, the science department got backed up by three weeks. So I figured I had three more weeks to run my project, and I kind of, you know, took my time on it. And then they said, 'Look, your deadline is up!' I'm like, what deadline? The science department is backed up, so what's the rush? Well, they let me go just because of that."

Julian then said slowly and dismissively, "Oh, yeah...well, that's just tough luck then, I guess." But he was thinking to himself, *For crying out loud, man, can't you keep it together enough to hold down a job?*

"Well, anyway," Drake said, "so how are things going at NASA?"

"Pretty good. Um, I've gotten promoted. I don't mean to rub it in your face now that you just got let go, but I got promoted…twice. They've been having me travel the country from one part of NASA to another—Silicon Valley, you know, Washington, Cape Kennedy, and so forth."

"Wow, sounds like things are going along swimmingly."

"Yeah, pretty all right," Julian replied uncomfortably.

"Well, maybe you can put in a good word for me there. You know I had great marks in college. You'd do that for me, right?"

Julian replied with hesitation, "Yeah, I'm sure they'll be very impressed with your scholastic achievements. All right, I'll put in a good word for you. Sure, I'll do that." But in his mind, he thought, *Damn, I really want to help him straighten up and fly right, but I just don't like the idea of risking the chance of hurting my reputation with NASA.*

So in an unsuccessful attempt to not be obvious, Julian redirected the conversation to small talk. Drake picked up on the camouflaged subtleties of Julian's redirection and reset the conversation to Julian's job at NASA saying, "So exactly what are you working on?"

After Julian gave Drake about a ten-minute, tour guide—inspired explanation of the comings and goings of NASA, their meals arrived. With platters in both hands, she placed Julian's in front of him first saying, "A steaming hot platter of snow crabs for you." And then looking at Drake, she said, "And a Three Mile Island platter of wings for you." She clasped her hands together and said, "Is there anything else you boys need?" They said no, thanked her, and began to eat their meals. Julian worked the snow crab eagerly, cracking, pulling, dipping, and devouring. Drake did the same, tearing into his wings and gulping beer with every other bite to satiate the fire in his mouth.

Not much was said from that point as Julian's lips and fingers were glazed in drawn butter, and Drake's were covered in red hot sauce as sweat began to bead across his forehead. After Julian tossed the last cracked, empty crab shell into the scrap bowl, he pushed his plate forward a few inches, leaned back, wiped his hands with a moist towelette, and said, "Damn, that hit the spot. I was starving."

Drake likewise leaned back in his chair, holding the last wing bone. He shot it basketball-style into the scrap bowl. He put both hands in the air and said, "He shoots. He scores!" He pointed a finger at Julian and said, "I'll bet I can score with our tasty waitress too!" Julian looked at Drake with a small grin, then looked over Drake's shoulder, and then back at Drake. Drake caught on and said, "She's standing right behind me, isn't she?"

Sally Sue let out a laugh and said, "Check please, I assume?"

"Yeah, check please," he said sheepishly. "Well, that makes for an awkward moment."

Sally Sue smiled at Drake and said, "Well, you are cute, and I am flattered, but one thing I'm not is easy." She set the check down on the table, smiled again, and quickly turned around and walked away.

Julian said, "Well, that was fun."

"You know, rejection is a powerful aphrodisiac."

"It is for you, I suppose."

"Well, that's easy for you to say, you lucky bastard. You've got Rebecca. I still can't believe she chose you over me to begin with."

Julian winced. "Ow, that's going to leave a mark. Thanks for the vote of confidence there, pal."

"Hey, I was just kidding. Look, you guys make a great couple. I just can't believe that she never even gave me a chance. But it doesn't matter. You two have been married for quite a while now. Do you want kids? Are you going to start a family at some point?"

Julian bit the side of his mouth a little and said, "That's been a bit of an issue, if you want to know the truth. We've been trying, and we're just met with disappointment month after month. We've both been checked out, and we know what the problem is. It's just that the doctors seem to think that the chances are slim, not impossible but slim."

"Well, if the problem is on your end, maybe I can help. I'd be more than happy to jump in the game and throw a few pitches."

Julian just stared at Drake for a moment with a look on his face that said, *You ass!*

"Hey, I'm just trying to help." After a long pause, Drake then said, "I'm sorry, man. I guess it was a poorly timed joke." Then in an attempt to move away from his verbal faux pas and navigate his way back to their premeal conversation, he said, "So you just gave me a generic outline of what NASA is all about, but you didn't really get into what you're doing there."

"Well, a lot of what I do, I'm not allowed to talk about, but I can give you the general scope. They have me working on a couple of projects. One is for specific flight patterns through space for potential upcoming missions, and they've got me working on the engineering side in the science department on the different mechanics of remapping the constructional aerodynamics of a space vehicle. But the one they're focused on the most is a project called M.O.M."

Drake said curiously, "Mom?"

"It stands for 'Man On Mars.' That's what they have at the forefront of their objectives. But what I'm most excited about is the one I talked them into. I'm attempting to bend light."

"What do you mean *bend light*? You mean to make an object seem to disappear like a cloaking device type of thing?"

"No, that's refracting light. We have people on that too, and they're getting a lot better at it as far as making things appear not to be there. But this is different. This is the actual bending of light, not redirecting it."

Drake said, "As far as I know, the only thing in the universe that can bend light is a black hole. How the hell are you going to duplicate that kind of power?"

"Well, first of all, that's why I call it the 'Black Hole Project.' It's not a matter of power actually. It's a matter of physics. You see, I'm using magnetic waves and radio waves to get ionized neutrons to interact together. The magnetic waves cause the neutrons to fold in on each other, and each time has a cascading effect to where the neutrons move faster and faster. The problem with the application, is, in order to keep the neutrons from just charging out into the atmosphere is to curve them into the shape of a bubble. This is where the radio waves come in. They interact with the magnetic waves at just the right frequency to start the circular cascading of the neutrons, and that is what allows the light or will allow the light to eventually, if I can get the neutrons to move fast enough, to actually bend."

Drake responded, "All right. That sounds very intriguing, but what uses would that have?"

"Well, there are all kinds. If I can make the bubble small enough, we can make a surgical instrument out of it so that doctors could be able to perform surgeries that prior might have been inoperable or other things like propulsion."

"Propulsion?"

"Yeah, even propulsion. It could change how people are able to travel, possibly even a power plant. And you know what? I really don't know what all the applications can be because if it works, it can be like the invention of plastic. I mean, who knew how many things could be made out of plastic when it was first produced? This sort of thing could have a multitude of uses. Remember when we were at MIT and I told you that creating a wormhole might be possible?"

Drake nodded his head. "I do remember that."

"Well, this is the 'Black Hole Project,' and it's not a stretch from that to perhaps create portholes for people to move about the earth without airplanes and to arrive at their destinations instantly! Imagine if you could just walk through a door and be in France. Walk through another door, and you're in China or wherever you want to be. Someday it could be tied into cell phones so people could just punch in a code and head off to anywhere! Imagine if you and I, instead of having this chance meeting where you still had to drive awhile, just called each other and said, 'I'll meet you in Atlanta for lunch in just a minute or Hawaii or wherever.' Imagine a guy gets off work, he and his wife have had a hectic day, and he calls her and says, 'Hey, let's meet for dinner in Belize, and maybe after that, we can go dancing at our favorite nightclub in Hong Kong!' I can see it, Drake. It's all possible. It's all right there!"

Drake with eyes wide-open said, "All that blows me away, and I understand the principles from which you've founded your theory, but how can you technologically bridge the gap between theory and reality?"

"Well, that's where NASA comes in. They build what I design. And between you and me, another part about creating a wormhole is time travel, and believe it or not, something like that would be easier to construct than a portal! I could probably do it myself."

"Time travel, really? Okay, now you're touching on the amazing, the unreal."

"Yeah, I think it has real potential. I'm excited about it. I haven't mentioned the time travel part to them yet. I don't want them to think I'm a whacko."

"I can relate to that. Let me know if you need any help. Seriously though, I'm going to put my resume in a couple of different departments. You'll put in a good word for me, right, man?"

Julian exhaled slowly and said, "Yeah, I will. I'll do it," thinking to himself, *All right. I will. I've given him my word. But damn it, I hope this doesn't blow up in my face.*

Julian pulled out his wallet and threw down a fifty-dollar bill on top of the check and said, "You drove, so this is on me, eight dollars on forty-two. That's what about nineteen percent?"

Drake said, "Actually, it's almost nineteen point one percent." A calculation shot through Julian's mind as he reached into his pocket to lay two pennies on top of the fifty dollar bill and said, "there, now it's exactly nineteen point one percent."

"Thanks for your two cents worth, Mr. Spock. Remind me to never doubt your calculations."

"Affirmative, Captain Kirk."

And with that, they stood and headed toward the door. Drake made his final quip as he opened the door to exit saying, "That poor Sally Sue doesn't know what she's missing out on." Julian just shook his head as he followed.

On the ride back to the airport, Drake said to Julian, "You know, I was actually hoping that I'd be able to ask you a favor."

"Name it. What do you need?"

Drake said, "I need to borrow a thousand bucks. I'm kind of low on cash. I've got rent due, and I've got a car payment."

"Okay, Drake. I can do that. But you haven't paid me for the last loan that I gave you."

"I know. I'll get around to it. I'm not going to forget. Besides, you're whacking down plenty of dough over at NASA. You can wait a little while, can't you? I mean, I'm not going to stiff you."

"No, it's not that. It's just that…"

"What?" Drake asked.

"It's just that… I don't know. I don't know. It's just that you could be doing a lot better right now. You have so much potential. You just need to get it together."

"Look, man, I need a little money. I don't need a lecture. I mean, not everybody is as lucky as you are. I'm having a tough time. That's all. Things will get better."

"Yeah, Drake, I'll loan you the money. But you know, even the way you think sometimes is a mystery to me."

"What do you mean the way I think?"

"Well, you just said that not everyone is as lucky as me. To tell me that I'm lucky suggests that I haven't earned anything."

"I didn't mean it like that. Of course, you've worked hard. You just make it look easy."

"It's all right," Julian said. "I'll cut you a check as soon as I get home and send it out. I've got so much going on with work, and we're moving soon too."

"Where are you moving to?"

"I'm moving back to Beech Grove actually. My mom is getting older, and she doesn't want to be alone, but she also doesn't want to live anywhere else. Since I travel around the country so much and do the rest of my work off of the computer, it pretty much means that I can live anywhere. And Beech Grove is home for me."

Drake said "That sounds ideal." as he pulled up to the sidewalk at the airport terminal, and they shook hands. Julian said, "It was good seeing you, man. You take care of yourself."

Drake said, "Likewise." It wasn't much of a good-bye as the tension from the earlier exchange was still fresh.

Julian slid out of the car, opened the back door, and grabbed his carry-on. He closed it and then looked back into the front door and said, "I'll see you around, buddy."

"You bet. And by the way, did you ever listen to 'An American Prayer'?"

"No, I actually haven't had the chance. But it's been on my to-do list."

"Yeah, do it sometime."

"I will. Take care now." He shut the door and made his way into the crowded airport.

Chapter 3

The Dead of Winter

A few weeks later, Julian and Rebecca rented a house just a few miles away from where his mother lived, and to his mother's delight, he had the old house bulldozed and a new one built. Just six months later, they moved in. It was a white two-story, colonial-style house with four bedrooms, three and a half baths, and a big front porch with a porch swing where Julian's mother could read, sip tea, or knit. And for Rebecca, there was a large back patio that overlooked a man-made pond that he had stocked with fish.

The following Saturday after moving in, Julian took Rebecca's SUV in for an oil change and tire rotation at Gabo's Garage. He paid his bill at the counter and walked out the front door which was located next to three auto bays. Standing at the end of bay two was an older, now-bald Ed Hansen. Julian didn't notice who he was for a second, but Ed did and said, "Well, look who it is, Mr. Big Shot!" Julian stopped to acknowledge Ed but thinking to himself, *I was hoping I would only have to run into this guy at class reunions.* But he offered him a greeting just the same.

"Well, hey there, Ed. How are you? Good to see you."

Ed folded his arms with a grumble and said only one word, "Bullshit!"

Julian said only one thing, "Oookay." Turning back in the direction of his SUV, he thought to himself, *No love lost there.* Ed paced in slowly behind him but at a distance. Julian, feeling the intimidation, just kept silent and turned the other cheek. Ed wanted to counter the cold shoulder and get a reaction. He stopped as Julian walked on.

"You think you own the world, don't you?" Julian just looked over his shoulder at him with a good-bye wave. He backed his car out and headed to the only exit, which caused him to pass by Ed still standing there on the way out. With one last attempt to get a rise out of Julian, he said, "Is your momma still hot?"

Julian just looked at him before pulling out and said, "Have a nice day… Eddie."

As he pulled away, he heard Ed shout in the distance, "Hey, nice rebuild on Lockwood. Looks like a great place!"

That comment gave Julian a bit of a chill. *I live on a dead end road, and I didn't even know he worked at*

Gabo's, but somehow he knew about my house? When he got back home, he told Rebecca about the encounter and not to worry. "I don't think it's any big deal, even though it was pretty stupid on my part to say what I said, but I don't think it's cause for concern. Sure does strike a man's nerve when you throw his mother into the mix like that. Dumb on my part though."

Rebecca, supportive as always, said, "Don't beat yourself up too much there, Mr. Not So Perfect. So he got to you, who cares? And trust me, I'm not worried at all. The doors have locks, and we have a gun! And you, sir, showed me how to use it properly, and for a girl, I'm as comfortable with it as any man, so no worries!"

Julian was a responsible gun owner and kept it where it could be easily accessed in case of an emergency but always kept it locked up if he knew that no one would be home.

During the time the house was being rebuilt, and thanks to Julian's influence, Drake had been working for NASA in Washington, DC, but had two negative reports on his official employee record. He had also already been demoted once.

Around dusk one autumn evening, Julian and Rebecca were sitting on the back patio by the pond which was surrounded by plush green grass and a dense cluster of trees. Through the branches and leaves, the light fading in the evening sky was casting flickering shadows across the pond.

They were sharing a bottle of wine. Julian had a round loaf of unsliced bread and was tearing off pieces. He was balling them up in his fingers and tossing them into the pond to watch the walleye and rainbow trout surface to grab their treats.

The patio deck itself was about fifteen by twenty feet, rectangular in shape and extended out from the back of the house over the pond, right off of the kitchen. It had a clear-stained natural wood that was lacquered to protect it from the elements. About half of it was built over the water's edge. Along the left-hand side, flower boxes lined the railing, and red perennials were in bloom. On the right, there was an L-shaped outdoor patio couch with cushions. The fabric was in many shades of green foliage and was perfect for the setting. In front of the couch was yet another rectangular butcher-block table that Rebecca shortened the legs of to match the height of the couch cushions. She had found it at a garage sale and knew it was going to be the perfect table for the little outdoor paradise she was creating. It was a wonderful reminder of her first date with Julian.

They were nestled together on the corner couch, Julian with his arm around her as she was laying sideways with her legs folded under. She was curled up onto his chest and said, "I wish I could stop time and make this moment last forever. This is truly my most favorite place in the whole world. I feel like the luckiest girl on earth that I get to spend it with you."

"Well, you sure know how to make a man feel like a man. I was just thinking about how good it feels to snuggle with you."

"You're too sweet," she said as she gave him a little peck on the cheek. She paused then and said, "What do you think we're going to look like when we get old?"

"I suppose gray-haired, wrinkled-up versions of what we look like now. I'll probably be fat and bald. Do you think you'll still love me then?"

"You'll always be my prince no matter what you look like when you're old. You'll always look handsome to me. And as long as you're by my side, we will be timeless. We'll be young forever."

Julian leaned forward and picked up both of the wine glasses. He gave Rebecca hers and said, "A toast to this moment in all of its perfection. May it last forever."

"I'll drink to that," she replied. "And you know what? One of the cool things about heaven is that after we grow old and die, we can come back and relive this moment as many times as we want."

Julian looked up as though he were thinking to himself but said out loud, "Note to self, come back and visit August twenty-eighth often!"

They each took a sip and then heard the sound of the bushes rattle from across the pond. "What was that? It was right over there," Julian said, pointing in that direction.

She responded playfully, "It was probably just a deer, my dear."

"A small one I guess." Then Julian smiled and said, "You know, the only thing missing from this Norman Rockwell painting," as he gestured toward an empty spot on the deck floor, "a toddler in a stroller right about there...maybe a little Rebecca."

"Or a little Julian," she replied. "But if we don't sometime soon, we can always adopt."

"I know. I'm not giving up either way," he said.

"That's good to hear because we've still got a lot of trying to do."

"Well," Julian said as he kissed the top of her head, "I guess there's a bright side to everything because trying sure is a hell of a lot of fun."

"Well, Mr. Phillips, Mrs. Phillips sure does like the way you try."

"What do you say we head upstairs and work on this problem?"

"Only if you can catch me first," she said as she quickly jumped up and scampered toward the kitchen door in her bare feet, holding the front of her summer dress up slightly as she ran.

"Oh, now we're playing hard to get, are we?" Julian said as he ran in behind her. Rebecca giggled as the chase was on.

The next morning, Julian awoke in their bed, lying on his back, nestled in their white satin sheets. Sunlight was shining through the window. Rebecca was still sleeping and laying on her side facing him. He gazed at her for a long moment and then slowly eased his way out of bed. It was a large square bedroom. Rebecca had chosen sky blue for the color, and it had beautiful white crown molding and white curtains. The walls were adorned with traditional and postmodern paintings. On the opposite side of the bed was a large picture window that overlooked the patio and pond. They had their own master bath and a workplace off to one side for Julian's desk and computers. He made his way over to it to check his emails.

Most of them were minor things to address, but then came one with the heading, "Trouble in DC." It was from the head of the science department in DC, Kevin Gerstner. It read, "Julian, just an FYI about your buddy Drake, he just isn't working out. He's frequently tardy and becomes indignant when confronted. This department needs teamwork, not arrogance. Sorry, but we have to let him go. This decision was reached last night in a closed-door meeting on August 28, that included the administrative director, the director of research and development, and myself. The termination is effective as of this morning, August 29. Drake will be notified upon his arrival."

Julian leaned back in his chair and folded his arms, lightly shaking his head. He said to himself sarcastically, "Big shock." He leaned forward and typed his reply. "Do what you must. Thanks for the heads-up. Julian."

The very next email was from the head project manager in Houston, James Daniel. The subject title was, "The Black Hole Project?" It read, "Julian, I'm sorry to inform you, but as you know, the Man on Mars project is consuming an enormous amount of resources. That, along with the budget cuts, has left us with no other choice but to cancel the Black Hole Project, for now anyway. We would like to revisit this in the future, but for now, it's just not in the cards. Again, I'm sorry. Sincerely, James Daniel."

Julian again leaned back in his chair, this time placing both of his hands with his fingers interlocked on top of his head. He let out a big exhale and said to himself aloud, "Holy crap. Last night, everything was all so good and full of hope and now this morning, two nuclear bombs in a row!"

*　*　*　*　*

A few days later, he was sitting at his brown oak kitchen table reading the morning newspaper with a cup of coffee and an uneaten piece of toast on a saucer in front of him. His cell phone, sitting on the table next to the toast, rang out Beethoven's Fifth (his favorite ringtone). He peered over the top of the newspaper and took a look at the screen. "Hmm… Drake." He was finally getting the call that he knew was coming sooner or later.

He popped his newspaper, folded it, and plopped it on the table. He picked up his cell phone, and just before pushing the answer button, he said to himself, "Okay, here it comes." Julian pressed the answer button and held the phone up to his ear, but he got no more out of his mouth than, "Good morning, Drake. I was going to—"

He was suddenly cut off by Drake blurting out, "Hola, amigo! Cerveza, por favor!"

Julian reacting said, "Ow, you don't have to shout. Damn, that's not exactly the good morning I was expecting!"

"That's because it's not morning where I am! It's still night."

"Well wherever you are, what the hell time is it there, amigo?"

"Let me see. Ah, it's just after four thirty. That means today is already tomorrow. Well then, good morning, señor!"

"Well, I'm no detective, but I'm guessing that by what time you're saying it is and that crappy Spanish accent that you're somewhere in Mexico. Am I right?"

"Si, señor. I'm in Cabo San Lucas doing the Cabo Wabo."

Julian replied with tolerant sarcasm, "And you chose me to be a part of your fiesta at seven thirty in the morning? I'm so pleased."

"Come on, Julian. Get happy! I'm celebrating!"

"Celebrating what?"

"I got canned, and I'm moving back to Indiana."

"Yeah, I got wind of that. I got an email a few days ago."

"I figured you probably would have heard about it by now. But we're going to be neighbors again!"

"Wow, looking forward to that," Julian said. "Well, do you have a job lined up? I mean, what's bringing you back to Indianapolis?"

"Well, what's bringing me back is an airplane, but nope, got no job lined up. I'm going to run this one by the seat of my pants."

"Nothing like having a plan, so when are you heading this way?"

"I'm gonna stay here in Cabo for a couple more days then I'm going back to DC to grab some of my shit, and then you'll have to come pick me up at the airport. And we'll celebrate."

"Well, then bring me a sombrero as a souvenir."

"Well, you'll have to remind me to do that. I've been drinking all day. I'm not going to remember any of this conversation at all."

Julian responded with, "Oh, well, thanks for saving me some time," as he held his cell phone out in front of his face and pushed the end button to dump the call.

He dropped his phone down on the table and picked up his piece of toast. Taking a bite, he said as he looked at his phone, "Drake, that's the most helpful information I've gotten from you in a long, long time."

Just at that moment, Rebecca came down the steps that led from the bedroom into the kitchen, wearing her light-green bathrobe. "Who was that?"

"That was *the beautiful mess.*"

"Does he need to borrow money again?"

"Hope not. He hasn't paid me back for the last two loans."

As Rebecca turned and opened the upper kitchen cabinet, she pulled down a coffee cup and said, "Well, what does he want?"

Julian folded his arms and looked at her intensely and said, "What does he want? He wants to be eighteen forever. He's moving back to southeast Indianapolis, and he's only going to be a twenty-minute drive from here. I get the feeling we're going to be seeing him a lot more frequently."

Rebecca said, "Well, he is fun to have around once in a while."

"Yeah, he's pretty entertaining if you take him in small doses."

* * * * *

About ten and a half hours later, Julian was sitting at the work desk in his bedroom, going over some more emails, and working on other science configurations for his Black Hole Project which he decided to undergo on his own. His mother shouted out from down the hall, "Julian, dinner will be ready soon!"

"Thanks, Mom. What's for dinner?"

She yelled out, "The Brady Bunch Special."

He chuckled and said, "Got it, pork chops and apple sauce."

Just then, Beethoven's Fifth sounded again. Julian looked down at his phone sitting right next to his keyboard. It was Julian's second call from Drake, but from Drake's perspective, it was the first. Julian answered the phone saying, "Hola, señor."

Drake in a far more somber and downtrodden voice replied, "Julian, how are you?"

"I'm good. The question is how are you?"

"Well, I guess, maybe by now you might have heard that I got canned from NASA."

"Yeah, I know. I heard about it."

"It wasn't my fault," Drake exclaimed. "I needed an extra day off, so I told them that I had pink eye. Simple enough, I figured."

"Let me guess. They wanted you to come in so they could confirm that you were sick?"

"They did, so I had to think fast. What I came up with was brilliant. I smoked a doobie, then put Visine in only one eye and *bam!* Instant pink eye!"

"They said you smelled like pot!"

After a pause to embrace his own stupidity, Drake said, "I guess I didn't think that one through."

Julian replied, "Maybe because you were stoned!"

"Umm…perhaps? Anyway, I'm on a little vacation, but I'm going to be moving back to Indiana soon."

"Really? You don't say."

"Yeah. Guess where I'm at right now?"

"Oh, I don't know. Let me think. If I were Drake, I'd probably go where the booze and women are cheap. So I'm going to guess Mexico, probably Cabo. Am I right?"

"Damn. How the hell did you know that? Do you have GPS on me somewhere?"

"No, just a lucky guess, and let me make a few more guesses. You're going to stay there a few more days, and then you're going to head back to DC, pick up some of your stuff. Probably no need for a moving van because most of your stuff is rented anyway, and then you're going to fly back to Indianapolis, but you're going to need me to pick you up at the airport. Is that about right?"

And then after a brief pause, Drake said, "Did I call you last night?"

"Well, it was your *last night*, but it was my *this morning*. But yeah, you called."

"Well, Kreskin, that goes a long way in explaining your psychic powers. But listen, I gotta go. My little señorita here needs my attention, and I'm going to give it to her. I'll give you a call in a few days when I get to DC and get my reservations booked."

"I might be out of town. If so, I'll send Rebecca to pick you up. But otherwise, safe travels. And don't forget my sombrero."

"Ummm…sombrero? Okay?"

"Well, adios, amigo."

* * * * *

A week later, Julian was taking care of business in Houston and sent Rebecca to pick up Drake, but before doing so, she needed to fuel up and grab a snack for the ride, stopping in at Bobba Lou's. As she was perusing the aisles, she landed her eye on some trail mix. When she leaned in to pluck her choice from the shelf, she noticed from the corner of her eye that someone landed their eyes on her. She didn't know his name but did know him as a homeless man that she had seen before on the roadside holding a sign that read, "Will work for food." She, like others, just gave him a donation and thought no more of it. Bill's lurking also caught the eye of Lou before it did Rebecca, and he was already moving in to deal with him. Rebecca was mid-aisle, and Bill was at the end and didn't see Lou coming because he was too busy peering at her. Lou snagged him by his soiled T-shirt sleeve, and Bill in a wobbled, surprised manner was pulled away.

Lou snapped at him in a sharp whisper saying, "Come on, Bill, you're being a little perv again."

"No, Lou, I'm just looking around is all."

"Looking for what? You don't even buy anything!"

Bill with a careless grin said.

"She sure is cute, ain't she? Ha!" That was all Lou needed to cup Bill's arm and shuffle him out the back door.

"That is the wife of a very good friend of mine. Now back off and stay out of my store!" He kept the encounter out of her view and then resumed his position behind the counter.

Shortly after, Rebecca approached saying, "Hello, Mr. Lou. How are you?"

"Good thanks."

Lou was curious to know if she was aware of Bill, so he asked an unusual question, "How was your shopping experience?"

"Well…a little creepy."

Lou tightened his lips before saying, "Yeah, I tried to head that off. Sorry about that."

"Not your fault, Lou, but thank you."

"It's what anyone would do, but I sent him on his way."

"I hope you weren't too hard on him. I would imagine it's not easy being a loner."

"I know, and I have sympathy for him, but my customers deserve to feel safe."

"Well, then you're my hero for today. But ya know I don't think he would ever harm anyone." Her eyes widened as she said, "But you never know, do you?"

"Nope! Can I get you anything else?"

"No, just this, and I have to get some gas. I'm headed to the airport."

"Picking up Julian?"

"No, one of his buddies from college, Drake Wallace."

"Never met him, but if he's a friend of your husband, he must be a good guy."

Rebecca, reacting to the thought of Drakes wild personality, laughed and said, "You never know do you. Take care Lou."

"You too. Drive safe." She exited with a chuckle. As she made her way to her car at the pumps, she noticed Bill in the distance, leaning against a tree and looking in her direction. It made her uncomfortable as he continued to stare the whole time she pumped gas. She felt a sense of relief when she pulled away to head for the airport. Once arriving, she waited outside of the gate. Drake was making his way through the crowded corridor with his carry-on backpack over his shoulder and a sombrero in his hand. He spotted Rebecca and smiled. He was wearing a blue, green, and white checkered flannel shirt, blue jeans with a hole in the right knee, and flip-flops. His hair was disheveled, and he had about five days' worth of unshaven growth on his face.

He greeted her with a hug and placed the sombrero on her head saying, "This is for Julian. And look at you! You're still just as beautiful as ever. You haven't changed a bit."

Rebecca smiled and said, "Thank you. And you… you look," as she stumbled to find the words. "You look as if you could use a shave!" Rebecca was wearing capris and a collared button-down sleeveless shirt. "But it's good to see you, Drake. It's been a long time."

"It's really good to see you too. You really do look fabulous.

I just need to make a quick stop over at baggage claim. I've got two pieces of luggage, and then we can be on our way."

Shortly after, Drake had loaded his luggage and backpack into the back of Rebecca's two-toned brown Cadillac SUV. As Rebecca was pulling out of the airport on her way to I-70, she said, "Okay. Where to, Drake?"

He replied, "2249 Lockwood Drive, Beech Grove."

"But that's my house," she replied.

"Yep, it sure is."

"Does Julian know this?"

"Nope. I thought I'd surprise him."

"Oh, he'll be surprised all right."

About the first five or ten minutes of the ride were mostly silent. Then Drake said, "I can't wait to see the new house."

"Yeah, I can't wait for you to see it either. It's really beautiful. Julian and I just love it there."

"So you and Julian are getting along pretty well?"

"Well, of course, we are. Why would you ask?"

"I don't know. Sometimes when two people have been together for a long time, some of the rivets start to rust. Some of the magic wears off. That's all."

"Not for us. We're just as in love with each other as we have ever been."

"Well, he's an awfully lucky man to have you."

"Well, thanks, Drake, but I also consider myself to be a pretty lucky girl."

Drake paused for a few moments and then said, "Do you mind if I ask you something rather personal?"

Rebecca said reluctantly, "Okay?"

"How come you never gave me a shot? You knew I was interested."

"Well, that is rather personal, but it's okay. You know the heart wants what the heart wants, and my heart just didn't want a relationship with you. It wanted Julian."

"Well, I was just talking about having some fun. You know, a few dates. I didn't really mean a relationship."

"Yeah, I know you didn't. And that's why I'm with Julian."

With a cocky smile and a cavalier manner, Drake said, "Well, Rebecca, if things ever do get stale and you feel like wandering off the reservation, keep me in mind."

Rebecca arched her eyes in surprise and replied, "Down, boy, down. My, you are a bold one. I'd tell you that I'm flattered, but I'm sure that would only encourage you. I'm very happy on the reservation, and I don't ever plan on leaving it."

"I was just kidding," Drake said unconvincingly.

After about ten seconds of awkward silence, Rebecca said, "Let's see what's on the radio."

The rest of their trip was just as devoid of conversation as it was when it began. Once they got back to the house, Rebecca set up Drake in their spare bedroom.

Two days later, Julian returned home. In that time, Drake had managed to behave himself. It was dusk, and the first cold wave of the coming winter season was crisp in the air. As Julian pulled in the driveway in his red BMW M6 coupé, Drake, awaiting Julian's arrival, made his way to the front door and down the front steps to greet him in the driveway. As Julian got out of his car and closed the door, he said, "Well, I see the prodigal son has returned."

"I have indeed." And they opened arms and gave each other a brief man hug.

Rebecca was standing in the doorway and said, "Enough frolicking, you two. I've been holding off on dinner, and I'm sure you're starved. Come eat."

Julian replied, "We're on our way, my lovely."

Drake said, "Any luggage?"

"Just the one piece here in the back."

"I'll grab it for you."

"Thank you, my good man." Drake pulled out the luggage, and they both made their way toward the front door.

In the cool fall evening and a short time after dinner, Julian and Drake retired to the back patio overlooking the lake, each with a cigar and a snifter of Hennessy XO. Drake commented, "Cognac. You've come a long way since college, Julian."

"Yeah, these days I enjoy a nice glass of liqueur about once a month or so, and then maybe two or three times a week, I'll have a glass of wine with dinner. Then during football season on a Sunday, I might even enjoy myself two or even three beers. I'm a real lush these days."

"Yeah, you're a real mess."

Julian said, "Yeah, a beautiful mess."

"What?" Drake asked, confused.

"Never mind. So how long are you staying?"

"Just until tomorrow morning. I've got a buddy from high school I was going to stay with for about a week, and he's lined me up with a little apartment that I can rent from month to month. But I kind of need a small loan, if you wouldn't mind helping me out a little bit. I hate to ask, but I'm flat broke."

"Flat broke?" Julian asked. "How can that be?"

"Well, Julian, flat broke is what happens when you're all out of money."

"Yeah, but how can you be flat broke? You just got back from Mexico."

"Yup. That's how I got flat broke."

"Well, how much did Mexico run you?"

"I don't know. Airfare, food, and accommodations, I guess a couple of grand. Why?"

"Well, I guess that couple of grand would have come in handy right about now. How much do you need to borrow? Probably a couple grand, I'm assuming?"

"Yeah, that would be about right."

"Drake, how can you keep spending money and then borrowing money? It just doesn't make sense. It's not responsible."

"Come on, man, you give me a speech every time I need a favor."

"Believe me, Drake, being the *keynote speaker* in your life is no fun either! And here I am being asked to give you money again. The last time I gave you a loan, you picked me up at the airport in a rented Hummer. How much did that run you, seventy, eighty bucks?"

"A hundred after the taxes and insurance. Why?"

"And how many days did you have it for?"

"Four days," Drake said.

"So that was four hundred bucks, and you borrowed a thousand from me. You could have borrowed six hundred or nothing at all if you didn't waste money like you do!"

"What the hell is wrong with me driving around in a nice Hummer? For crying out loud, you've got a Beemer, and your wife drives a Cadillac!"

"You just don't get it, Drake, do you? I earned them. We can afford them. That's why we drive those vehicles."

Drake snapped back, "Okay, Mr. Perfect. Thanks for nothing. I'll pack my shit and be gone first thing in the morning." And with a backhanded slap, he knocked over his snifter of cognac as he stormed away.

As the back door to the kitchen slammed shut, Julian looked down at the spilled snifter of cognac and mumbled to himself, "Nice. Real mature dumb ass." He felt that Drake needed a wake-up call and thought it best to leave it as it was, thinking in his attempts to help Drake, he was only enabling him.

The next morning, he found that for the first time, Drake had made good on his word and was gone.

* * * *

Three months later in the dead of winter, Julian was sleeping in after having taken a red-eye flight back from Silicon Valley the night before. He was awakened by the sound of Rebecca singing "Happy" by Pharrell. His eyes squinted at first and then opened fully to find her standing over him with a tray for breakfast in bed.

As she sang the lyrics, "Clap along if you feel like a room without a roof. Clap along if you feel like happiness is the truth!" she placed the tray over him, straddling his body, saying, "Good morning, sunshine. I have for you two eggs over easy, just the way you like 'em, sausage links, your favorite homemade hash browns, my specialty. And then there's also a lightly buttered English muffin and orange juice with pulp. I would have included a flower from the garden, but they're buried under a foot of snow."

Julian looked at her questioningly. "Let's see. It's not my birthday."

"Nope, not yours."

He said, "It's not your birthday either."

"Nope, not mine."

"It's not our anniversary."

"Nope, none of the above. But I got you a present just the same." She handed him a gift that was about the size of a clothespin and wrapped in white paper with a small red bow.

As he began gently tearing at the paper to unwrap it, he said, "But I didn't get you anything."

She said, "Well, you kind of did, but this gift is for both of us, Daddy."

"He bolted straight up into a sitting position with a wide-eyed look of shock and said, "What do you mean?" as he began feverishly tearing at the paper. He found a pregnancy test with a plus sign.

Julian in a rare moment of feeling at a loss for words stammered saying, "We…we…we are? "I… I mean… you are? We…us…a baby?"

Rebecca, delighted by his surprise, grinning from ear to ear, said, "Yes, you silly. Yes, we, us, baby, yes, all of the above."

Julian quickly grabbed the tray and set it aside as quickly as he could without spilling the orange juice, and then he shot out of the bed, hugging Rebecca as though he had never hugged her before. He put his hands on either side of her head, kissed her, and then kissed her again, and then a big hug, and another kiss. Then he started pacing back and forth nervously and excitedly announcing a to-do list. "We have to get…we have to get a crib, and we have to get a bassinette…and a stroller, and we've got to convert the extra bedroom.

And we've got to paint the walls pink or blue. Do you know? Is it a boy or a girl?"

Rebecca, with her hands clasped against her chest, giggled as she watched his frantic reaction and said, "Take it easy, Julian. Take it easy. I can do all the nesting myself. We have plenty of time."

Julian paused at the foot of the bed and looked at Rebecca with glazed eyes and said, "You're right. You're going to be the best mom ever," and then he walked over and gave her another hug, but this one was slow and warm.

"Oh God, I so don't want to leave on Monday. I hate leaving you behind as much as I do to start with, but now with this news, I really don't want to go." Then he paused for a moment and said, "You know, I've got an idea. Since I've got to go down to the Kennedy Space Center on Monday and I've got to be there for about two weeks, why don't you and Mom fly down with me for at least a week? Thaw out for a little while. What do you think?"

With her arms around his waist, she slid her hands up the length of his back until they came to rest on top of his shoulders. She leaned her head back and attempted to make a serious face, looked into his eyes and said, "You want me to leave the frozen tundra and go and spend a week on a beach in sunny Florida? I don't know. I guess a successful marriage is about sacrifice now and then. Well, all right. I guess you're worth it." They were both grinning as he used his bear hug to pick her up off the ground a few inches and then put her back down and gave her another long kiss.

Julian had booked round-trip tickets for himself, Rebecca, and his mother for the full two weeks, but because of the extra time that he spent with the two of them, he was forced to remain an extra three days to complete his work as his loved ones returned home. Whenever Julian was away on business, he always called home at least once a day, and on the morning of his final day before his return home, he made his call. It went unanswered. While it wasn't unusual that Rebecca would miss a call from time to time, she would always ring him back promptly. An hour later, another call went unanswered, and half an hour after that, another call unanswered. After the fourth unanswered call, he called his mother once and then a second time, and it was the same—no answer. Just before his plane departed, he called Deputy Scott and asked him to roll by the house for a quick look saying, "I'm sure everything is fine, but I'm just a little worried. That's all." Scott said that he would and not to worry.

Once his plane landed at the Indianapolis International Airport, Julian immediately called once again and got no answer. Julian's worry had turned to fear, the kind of fear that made him feel sick in the pit of his stomach. He knew that something was wrong, very wrong. His calls had never gone unanswered for this long, much less by both his mother and his wife. He tried time and time again to convince himself that it was just a coincidence and that everything was actually fine. Trying desperately to believe his own reassurances, he sped along faster down the icy roads. It seemed like the road itself was growing longer and longer as he went. He felt as if he would never reach his destination, as though he was chasing the horizon.

After what felt like an eternity, he finally reached Lockwood Drive and though the house was still out of view, in the distance, he could see red-and-blue lights reflecting off the snow banks at the mouth of his driveway. He felt his heart drop into his stomach. His hands and feet went numb, and his body felt as cold as the frozen roads that led him there. His lower lip quivered as he mumbled aloud in a broken voice, "No, God, no. Tell me they're all right. Tell me they're all right. No, God, please!"

A sharp and hasty left-hand turn into the driveway caused the rental car to slide into the snowbank on the right side of the cobblestone drive. He quickly attempted to exit the car, but the door only opened a few inches as it had jammed into the snow. He threw a hard shoulder into the door and then again a second time, allowing the door to open just enough for him to squeeze out and begin his forty-yard panicked sprint toward the front of the house where four Marion County police cars with flashing lights lined the circle.

Yellow police tape streamed across the front patio, and parked in the front yard to the left was a white van that was marked "Beech Grove Crime Scene Unit." As he ran ever closer, the house itself seemed as though it was moving backward away from him. As his heart pounded like a jackhammer in his chest, cold, white breath poured from his nostrils as he shouted, "No, no, no!" Two officers collided with Julian in an effort to stop him from breaking through. A third officer also came to assist. It was Officer Scott.

"Julian, don't. Don't do this."

"That's my family! What happened? What happened?" Julian's face was beet red, veins around his eyes, forehead, and neck protruding as he frantically struggled with all of his might to free himself from their grasp. He wedged his right arm between them over the top of their shoulders, stretching his hand as far as he could, grasping at thin air in a desperate attempt to reach the house.

Officer Scott pleaded with him in a loud but sympathetic voice, "Stop, Julian, please stop. There's nothing you can do."

With desperation of breath, Julian said, "What do you mean there's nothing I can do? What are you trying to say?"

"I'm sorry, Julian. I am so sorry, but they're gone."

Julian's eyes were bloodshot and swollen as the tears poured down his face. He shouted, "Shut your filthy mouth, you goddamn liar! They're not gone!" And his body went limp as he dropped to his knees, fists planted in the snow. He said over and over, "She's not gone. She's not gone. She's having my baby. She's going to have my baby. She's not gone. She's not gone." His loud acclamation grew quieter and quieter each time he said, "She's not gone."

Officer Scott knelt in the snow beside him with his hand on his back rubbing in a circular comforting way. "I'd give anything to change this, my friend. I am so sorry. I'd give anything to change it. God bless you, Julian. I am so sorry." Officer Scott stood and slowly backed away, motioning to the other two officers to back away as well to give Julian time to console himself.

A few moments later, without saying a word, Julian sprang from the ground and charged toward the door. Officer Scott shouted, "Julian!" as he followed in pursuit behind him. As Julian burst through the door to the right and about twenty feet in, he could see the first white sheet-covered body, bloodstained at the head. He carefully knelt and began to pull back the sheet.

Officer Scott, noticing another two officers in the house moving to deal with Julian, told them, "Stand down, gentlemen. Leave him be."

He continued to pull back the white sheet. It was his mother, barely recognizable. Her face was swollen from having been bludgeoned in the back upper portion of her skull. Weeping and shaking, he placed his hands on either side of her face saying, "Momma, Momma, my dear sweet Momma." Tears upon tears poured down his face as he moaned. He leaned back on his knees and carefully replaced the white sheet over her face. He put his hand over his mouth and the other on the floor to help himself stand, his head swirling with emotions, his body swaying as he stood.

He turned toward Officer Scott who was still standing in the doorway. With a look of drunken exhaustion, Julian shook his head slightly from side to side and asked, "Where's Rebecca?"

Scott said nothing as he directed with his eyes and a slight nod gesturing in the direction of the staircase. Julian made his way slowly at first and then quickened his pace until he got to the top of the stairs where he paused, took a deep breath, and headed toward the master bedroom.

The door to the master bedroom was wide-open with one police officer standing just outside. He looked at Julian and then hesitated a moment as Sheriff Scott came up behind Julian and motioned for the officer to let him pass. Julian's body was completely numb in a dreamlike state. He felt as though he was floating. As he entered the room, he saw the second white sheet covering the victim on the bed. Knowing that it was Rebecca that lay beneath, he paused with a glazed stare as though he was possessed by a spirit.

He gently reached out his arms, his hands trembling about a foot above her body as though he were addressing a hallowed altar. The two crime-scene investigators in the room, each clad in navy-blue dress pants with white long-sleeve shirts and badges fixed to their belts, took leave of their duties and left the room in reverence to Julian's mourning.

Sheriff Scott was standing just inside the doorway and said, "Are you sure you can handle this?" Julian, sobbing, gave no reply. After a pause, Julian gently pulled back the sheet to see Rebecca's angelic face. She looked as though she were merely sleeping.

Julian, weeping, said in a low, soft voice, "Oh, my love, my dear sweet Rebecca. What have they done to you? I love you. I love you. I love you." He gently cupped her face in his hands and then leaned in and gave her a hug and a kiss on the side of her cheek and then gently rocked back and forth with the occasional moan.

After about two minutes, Julian composed himself enough to stand, wiping the tears from his eyes and never taking them off of her. He knew that Scott was in the room and asked, "I don't see any signs of blood on the sheet. How did she pass?"

For a moment, Scott searched for a way to answer gently and sympathetically, then said, "It appears to be asphyxiation."

"Are there any signs that she suffered before that?"

"There are rope burns on her wrists. Her hands were tied at one point, likely behind her back."

With a lump in his throat, Julian timidly asked, "Was she raped?"

"We won't know for sure until forensics come back. We're going to have them work through the night, if necessary. But we don't think so because there wasn't much sign of a struggle other than the rope burns. But we did find her there on the bed completely disrobed."

Julian was physically and emotionally drained. Scott offered for him to stay the night at his place saying, "We'll know more in the morning, and I'd rather tell you in person than over the phone." Julian agreed.

* * * * *

The next morning, Julian would find himself even more exhausted, having tossed and turned most of the night. What little sleep he did get was marred by nightmares and unwanted visions of how it might have happened. Julian and Scott sat across from each other in the kitchen of Scott's humble abode. Scott, sipping his coffee, was no longer in uniform but wearing a simple pair of blue jeans and a white short-sleeve undershirt. Julian's cup sat on the table in front of him untouched. Very few words were shared between the two of them. Scott could not find the words to ease his friend's pain. He thought to himself, *How can I console a man who has lost so much? And small talk is out of the question.* A deafening quiet ruled morning the air.

But the stillness of the hour would not last as the ring of Scott's cell phone sharply cut through the silence. He answered, "Sheriff Scott here." It was the coroner's office. He stood and walked out of the room to take the call. After about ten minutes, Scott walked back in and returned to his seat across from Julian. He placed his elbows on the table, interlocking his fingers, looked at Julian, and said, "That was the coroner's office."

Julian, weary eyed and pale, simply asked with almost no emotion, "What did they say?"

With great trepidation, Scott said, "In the case of your mother, as we already surmised, she died from a single blow to the back of her head."

"Did she suffer for long?"

"No, she didn't, Julian. She died instantly."

"And Rebecca?"

Scott paused for a moment and said, "Yes, Julian. She did die of asphyxiation, and the killer used the plastic bag that we found next to the bed by the window." Scott placed his hands on the table and nervously tapped his fingers before he said, "And there's one more thing that you should know, and I hate to tell you."

"What is it? Tell me."

Tapping his fingers again, he said, "She was…she was raped."

"But how can that be? You said she didn't struggle," Julian said sharply. "I don't believe that for a second. She would have fought with everything in her to prevent herself from being raped."

"I know that she would have, Julian, and there's no easy way to put this, but the rape was postmortem."

Julian felt gut punched as his sorrow and remorse was overtaken by an all-consuming rage that boiled as it coursed through his veins. He stood quickly, anger pulsing, ears ringing, vision distorted as he jeered with his mouth agape. He clenched his fists and paced back and forth. He spoke aloud as though he were alone in the room. "How could someone do that? Evil, it's just pure evil. How can you use my wife as though she was your play toy, like she was some piece of trash that you could use and discard? How could you do that? You evil son of a bitch. I'm going to get my hands on you, and I'm going to kill you, you evil son of a bitch."

Scott said, "Easy, Julian, easy. Be careful of what you say. No one is above the law. I know you're angry, but please be careful of what you say. I'm... I'm just going to pretend I didn't hear that."

Telling Scott what he wanted to hear, Julian said appeasingly, "You're right. You're right. I didn't mean that. It was just anger coming out." But the thought still echoed in his head.

In Scott's mind, he knew what Julian really meant but thought that if he were in Julian's shoes, he would feel no different. In an attempt to shift the conversation away from what he had said, Julian asked, "So is there any evidence or DNA or anything that might provide a lead?"

Scott, feeling powerless and frustrated, looked toward the ground and said, "No. No, there was no evidence at all. Gloves were used. No DNA evidence. A condom was used, and her body was cleaned meticulously. Not even a single hair was found, and they ran each test twice. But that doesn't mean the investigation will end, and it doesn't mean that we won't eventually crack the case. Evidence pops up sometimes days, weeks, months, even years after a crime is committed. It seems like the work of a serial killer, but all things are a possibility at this point. So the next question is, is there anyone that comes to mind?" There wasn't a split second between Scott's last word and Julian's first.

"Ed Hansen! You need to question him!"

"Won't be the first time we've done that, but why him?" Julian explained the verbal conflict at Gabo's that caused his suspicion. Then Scott said, "Well, that certainly is good enough of a reason to bring him in, and when it comes to that guy, all I need is a reason, doesn't even have to be a good one. We've brought him in for questioning several times over the last ten years or so, including a murder rap and a suspicious death. Nothing ever stuck to him though. Anyone else you know that could have been acting funny or strange lately, anything at all?"

Julian reviewed his mental search for a suspect and said, "She did mention that homeless guy a couple of times. You know, the burly one?"

"You mean old Bill Watkins?"

"Yeah, I guess that's his name. I don't know, but I just see him around town all the time."

"Well, what about it?"

"I don't know. Some months ago, she said that he was giving her the creeps. She was at Bobba Lou's shopping and said he was lurking around the aisles, staring her up and down. And then when she left, he was there in the parking lot watching her. She pretended not to notice. She just said that he gave her the creeps, but I don't know. He seems like a harmless guy to me, but you never know I suppose."

Then Scott said, "Well, we'll definitely round him up and ask him some questions. He does have one lewd and lascivious on him and an indecent exposure, a couple of petty thefts. But he just doesn't seem smart enough to be able to pull off something like this. But nonetheless, no stone unturned. We'll look into it."

"Well, I'll put some more thought into it obviously, but nothing comes to mind right now. But what if it is a serial killer? What then?"

"Well, if it's a serial killer, then it's a whole other ball game. We might be able to find similarities from another crime scene and link it to this one, but it could be somebody that's just roaming the country looking for opportunities. It would take a stroke of luck, if that's the case. But in the meantime, I've got to get down to the station. You're welcome to stay here as long as you'd like."

"No, I appreciate your hospitality a lot, but I think for now I'm just going to get a hotel room. I have to put the pieces together and figure out what I'm going to do from here."

Officer Scott went on his way, as did Julian.

Later that day, Julian received a call from his old friend Drake with words of sympathy and condolences as well as regret for the way he behaved when last they spoke.

Because of Julian's prominence at NASA, the double murder made national news. In the coming days, people would pour in from all over the country to attend the funeral, old friends of Julian's from high school and MIT as well as coworkers from NASA, and Rebecca's extended family and friends. Friends of Julian's mother were in attendance as well as old relatives.

Before, during, and after the funeral services, Julian put on an act, giving the appearance to all that he was holding up as well as could be expected under the circumstances. But on the inside, Julian was far from all right. He was falling apart.

He was grateful to everyone who came to pay their respects, but by the end of the service, he just wanted to get through the massive line of mourners and well-wishers. And at the very end, the very last one, and not by accident, was Drake. He embraced Julian with a hug, tears and sorrow.

He said, "Julian, when I got the word, I was shocked. I am so sorry this happened to you, and I know you've heard it from probably everyone, but if there's anything I can do, if you need me to stay with you for a while, if you need me to pick something up from the store, if you want me to do anything at all, I'm here for you."

Julian was grateful and knew that Drake meant it. "Thank you. Thank you, my friend, and I know you mean it. And to tell you the truth, I wish that everyone here could do something for me if for no other reason than that they could feel like they were being helpful in some way. But there truly is nothing that anyone can do for me. And for right now, I think I need to be alone. I'm just going to be by myself for a while."

"Do you really think that's a good idea?" said Drake.

"I don't know anything anymore. I just feel like being a lone soldier," he said. "You're more than welcome to come by and stay the night. But in the morning, please be on your way. I mean no disrespect, but I'm just going to need solitude."

"You don't need to explain or apologize, Julian. I completely understand, and I'll respect your wishes."

When they got back to Julian's house, he pointed to the downstairs bedroom that belonged to his mother as well as the master bedroom upstairs. Both had been sealed off, never to be used again.

Drake said, "It's got to bother you staying here in the house with all the memories. How do you deal with the pain?"

"I don't. And as for memories, right now I don't want to forget." He then said, "Come with me," and motioned for him to follow. He led Drake into the kitchen, reached into the lower cabinet, and pulled out a half-empty bottle of Hennessy XO. Then from the upper cabinet, he pulled out two snifters. He held them up and said, "Join me."

Drake said, "No, thanks. I'm good. I think I'm just going to sit this one out."

"Really?" Julian said with a raised eyebrow. "What gives?"

"I don't know. I'm just not feeling it right now." Drake was thinking that it would be a bad night for him to start drinking and not be able to stop. Drinking always made him want to celebrate and he knew that was not what Julian needed. "And besides, the world needs to catch up to me. If I never drink another drop, I will still have drank more than the average man! But don't let me stop you."

"That's unusual...unusual indeed," Julian said as he poured himself a shot. It had taken him six months to drink half of that bottle of Hennessey but only four hours to consume the remainder. Julian had done something he had never done before in his entire life; he got drunk. As the night proceeded, the irony of the role reversal was apparent to both but mentioned by neither.

The next morning, Julian would awake to find himself on the living-room couch, disheveled and groggy and still wearing the same clothes from the night before. And he would also quickly realize another sensation that he had never experienced before…a hangover. He stood slowly and then sluggishly made his way to the kitchen for a cup of joe. Drake had already prepared a pot, and to the left of the coffee maker, there was a white coffee cup, two Tylenol, two vitamin B12, and a note. The note read simply, "Julian, as self-appointed veteran of the hangover wars, I knew that you would need these. Sincerely, Drake."

Julian gave a slight smirk that looked more like a grimace, poured himself a plain, black cup of coffee, and set it on the kitchen table. He walked back across the kitchen and opened the cabinet directly above the refrigerator and pulled out a Colt .45 snub-nose revolver that he once kept in the safe that was hidden behind the nightstand in the master bedroom. He walked back to where his coffee was, sat down, and placed the gun on the table in front of him. He picked up the coffee cup and held it in both hands. With his elbows on the table, he stared at the gun, never taking his eyes off of it. He took a sip and began to have a conversation with the weapon.

"What are we going to do with you today?" He took another sip. "What are we going to do with you? She needed you, and you let her down." He continued to stare for a long moment, took another sip, and said, "You weren't there for her. Things could have been different. You could have saved her, but you couldn't because I locked you away. She was unable to reach you." Another sip. "Things could have been so different, but you... I let her down." His voice was slow and methodical, like that of a man on the verge of a descent into madness. He said to the weapon, "Maybe you can end my pain right now. Maybe that's what you're here for." He set his coffee cup down, picked up the gun with both hands, and placed the barrel in the very center of his forehead. With his right thumb on the trigger, he slowly began to squeeze, then stopped and said, "I'm going to let God decide this one."

He brought the gun down from his forehead, opened the cylinder, and allowed the bullets to spill out onto the table. He then picked up one single bullet and returned it to the cylinder, closed it, and spun it. He returned the barrel of the gun to the center of his forehead, and again with his right thumb, he squeezed until metal hit metal. The gun clicked, and no bullet fired.

He put the gun back down on the table and set it among the scattered bullets. He looked skyward and said, "If that's your decision today, so be it. But I'll let you decide again tomorrow."

Chapter 4

Darkness

The days that followed would prove to be very difficult for Julian, more so with each and every hour that passed. At the insistence of James Daniel in Houston, NASA requested that Julian take grief counseling with which Julian complied.

One of the components of the counseling required that he keep a daily journal of how he was doing emotionally. He kept two journals. In one, he wrote the things that he knew they would interpret as progress, as healing. But he was not healing. He wrote things that they would see as acceptance. But he was not accepting.

He began to feel suffocated with depression and enveloped in anguish. In the second journal that he kept at his house and allowed no one to see, he wrote the same thing each and every day, *"I spit with anger and clench my fists. I curse my God and beg him why. Be gone with life, I long to die."*

Each day that went by, it became a ritual. He would write that same passage and then put the barrel of the gun back to the center of his forehead, and for the seventh day in a row, the gun just clicked.

With six possibilities in the game of Russian roulette, Julian was now beating the odds. And he had given his gun a nickname. He referred to it as *Darkness*. And each day before he began his macabre routine, he would hold the gun and stare at it, sometimes up to an hour as memories of his wife and his mother would flow through his mind much the way tears would flow from his eyes.

He looked down at his revolver and said, "Hello, *Darkness*, my old friend." And in his head, a song by Simon and Garfunkel played over and over again, "The Sound of Silence."

> *"Hello darkness my old friend. I've come to talk with you again. Because a vision softly creeping. Left its seeds while I was sleeping, and the vision that was planted in my brain, still remains within the sound of silence."*

And now two days shy of two full weeks since the day of the funeral, the scruffy-faced, unshaven Julian would beat the odds once again. But the thirteenth day would be different than the previous twelve. On this day, after he spun the cylinder once again, he was gently rocking back and forth, sobbing and holding the gun in both hands. He thought to himself, *I've beaten the odds by double, but today is 13, unlucky 13.* And at that moment, a line from that song stood out in his head.

"And the vision that was planted in my brain, still remains."

Those words, "The vision that was planted in my brain, still remains," caused him to remember something that he said to Rebecca. He told her that after he died, he would often return to visit August twenty-eighth. And that thought led him to another—The Black Hole Project and possibility of time travel.

He stood up abruptly with a look on his face that was a cross between intense pondering and that of a man who had just found something that he had lost. He wiped the tears from his eyes with the sleeve of his gray robe. He set the gun down on the table and reached out, his hands and arms skyward in a pose of angelic praise and said, "My God! I can revisit the past, and I can change it! She'll always be there, and she'll always be young and beautiful, preserved in time!"

He then dropped to his knees and clasped his hands together and said the Lord's Prayer. He continued to pray saying, "God, forgive me. For twelve days straight, by the sound of the gun's hammer, you told me that it was not my time to die. With all that is in me, I believe that I can create a wormhole. I can find her somewhere in time. Please help me to make it so that she never died! And if I fail, I will mourn her all of the days of my life, but if you would help me, perhaps I can find peace."

He concluded with an amen and the sign of the cross. He stood and looked at the gun and said, "Oh Darkness, oh, I need to keep you away from me." He shook his head gently saying, "You are a poisonous snake that could have bitten me!" He continued to look at the revolver for a long moment and wondered what the result would have been had he not remembered his promise to Rebecca.

And then he picked up the gun, pointed it away from his body, and pulled the trigger. And with a mighty blast, it blew a hole in the kitchen wall.

He dropped the gun in shock. His eyes were wide-open as though he had just been awakened by fire, realizing the gravity of the chances that he had taken. He then stared at *Darkness* there on the floor for what seemed like a full minute, held out his hand, and with a circular motion as though he were purging a demon, he said, "No more! Be gone with you! You have power over me no more!"

He then took his fist and pressed it against his lips and began to think, began to ponder. He paced back and forth through the kitchen and then through the living room and back into the kitchen with no direction of purpose as he roamed aimlessly. Only mathematical thought and possibility entered his mind. Then he thought of how he could pick up where he left off with the Black Hole Project at NASA and if he could somehow go it alone.

Julian wasted no time. He immediately began studying up on the works of Nikola Tesla as well as Walther Gerlach, the scientist who worked for Hitler on what was known as *Hitler's bell*. Although there was no direct evidence that Nikola Tesla was successful in his attempt to time travel, there was speculation that Hitler's bell actually did work. He not only found striking similarities between both of those projects but also similarities in his own work.

*　*　*　*　*

When the time came, he sought the help of James Daniel. Although James was unaware of the exact purpose of Julian's work, he was more than happy to help, especially in light of what had just recently happened to Julian's family. Knowing that NASA would not officially fund the project, he saw nothing wrong with him pursuing it on his own. Julian began gathering leftover parts and pieces of this and that from the various divisions of NASA around the country. He centralized his efforts in Houston. And because of his position of power, no one beneath him recognized his independent work. Those above him felt he was likely trying to keep himself busy. They, too, had respect for him and his recent losses. Julian was able to construct a box that would hold the energy necessary to attempt to create a vortex. The box was silver in color and made of titanium alloy. It was rectangular and about the height of a grocery cart and twice the width. The top of the box was made with bulletproof glass for easy viewing. Affixed to each of the long ends of the box was a mixture of tubes, wires, and power cords. It looked like something that was a cross between what you might see on *Star Trek* and what you might find in *Sanford and Son*'s backyard. Also on the long ends of the box but on the inside were what looked like tuning forks, twenty rows of three on each end. After completing construction, he had given it a name, just as he had with his Colt .45. He called the box Pandora. The initial experimentation with Pandora went more or less as Julian had anticipated. But trial and error would provide him with the knowledge he needed to advance his mission. By causing ionized neutrons to rotate in the center of the box, Julian was able to create a bubble about the size of a walnut that was metallic blue in color. Eventually he was able to control the size of the bubble, but for practical purposes, he kept it to about the size of a volleyball. He used the vibration of radio waves to control the bubble. Higher frequencies would cause the bubble to create a vortex tail that would shoot sharply to the right. Lower frequencies would cause the vortex to shoot to the left. He knew that one meant forward in time and the other meant backward, but which was which, he had no idea. In an effort to discover what was forward in time and what was backward, Julian decided to attempt to put a timepiece in the center of the bubble.

For this, he decided to use a woman's Timex wristwatch because it was small. The face was about the circumference of a dime. He removed its brown leather straps, and with a string, he suspended the time piece from the inside lid of Pandora. Julian set the hour, minute, and second hand all at twelve o'clock and closed the lid. Then he initiated Pandora. As soon as the bubble was created, it immediately cut the string. However, the timepiece did not fall through the bottom of the metallic sphere. After a few seconds, the bubble became unstable and collapsed in on itself, melting the watch, which then dropped to the bottom of Pandora.

Julian had discovered that matter contained within the bubble altered the harmonics that allowed the cascading effect of the neutrons. He surmised that additional radio waves could be the answer, but it took another six months of painstaking trial and error before he was able to resolve the problem. During that time, he caused the meltdown of several hundred watches.

Julian suspended watch number 337, much the same as he had the previous 336, but this time, the bubble remained stable. Curious and cautious, Julian studied the bubble for about twenty minutes, recorded, and made notations. Once he felt comfortable enough, he turned the radio frequencies high, creating the vortex tail that shot sharply to the right. At that moment, the metallic blue orb turned metallic black and vanished, watch and all.

"Yes!" Julian exclaimed loudly as he gave a fist pump and then smacked his hands together saying, "Hot damn, hot damn! Yes, yes, yes!" And then he smacked his hands together again.

He then paused because he was puzzled. He placed his hand up to his chin, tapping his lips with his index finger as it occurred to him that he was uncertain about what he had just done. He felt certain that he didn't send the watch back in time because if he had, it would likely appear as though the bubble had never left. So forward in time must be the answer, but where? Or more specifically, when?

Julian waited several hours. Eventually he put Pandora back in the storage closet where he locked it up at night, but he remained in the lab, waiting and wondering. He patiently kept vigilance in his office chair, staring in the direction of where Pandora had launched the orb from.

He began to nod off until he heard that electrical hum that the orb would make when initiated. He looked up quickly to see the black metallic ball appear three feet above the ground, faded, and then the watch dropped from midair to the ground as the orb dissipated.

He quickly noted, five hours, twenty-three minutes, and approximately thirty seconds. He rushed over and picked up the watch to discover that only a few seconds had ticked by. Holding the watch in his right hand, he gently closed his fingers over it into a fist. A tear fell from his eye as he softly said, "I'm coming, Rebecca. I'm coming, my love."

* * * * *

From that point on, Julian's objective was to create a self-contained craft that could move back and forth through time without the reliance of Pandora. Until now, few at NASA had any knowledge of Julian's work because Pandora was small, and he kept it locked away at night and also because he was working on the Black Hole Project in his spare time. No one that knew he had a side project had any idea what his purpose for it was. But he knew that if he was to take his work to the next level, he would no longer be able to fly under the radar and would have to continue his experiments at home. From his garage, he began laying out the framework of a time machine about the size of a go-kart, flat and low to the ground, made of titanium alloy as was Pandora. It sat on four pegs about two feet above the ground. Not knowing what type of situations he might encounter in time travel, he constructed the machine to be folded in half so that it could be carried somewhat easily.

Julian's uncle on his mother's side, Bill Cox owned the Indiana Precision Grinding Company in Indianapolis. It was formerly a tool-and-die shop where Julian could have specialized parts made. Though his uncle had no clue what each of the parts were used for, he was glad to be part of the mystery, occasionally joking, "I've got another piece of your space shuttle, Julian. I'll mail it out."

Julian took a leave of absence from NASA to further focus on his quest. From his garage, he would often work from sunup until sundown, carefully designing and assembling the various pieces of the time machine that he named Pandora II but quickly began to refer to it simply as Pandora.

The one-year mark of the passing of his wife and mother was the date that he had set as his deadline, but his work took him six months past the date of that grim anniversary. Finally, Julian completed the construction of Pandora II. Still sitting on four pegs, it was about half the length of a gurney, and on the sides from front to back, curling in an upward position, was the tuning fork-looking particle feeders.

Julian had found that quartz within the watches had increased the harmonics of the particle feeders, and he lined the floor of the craft with this precious crystal. It acted as a giant synopsis for the cascading effect of the neutrons. There was a seat that was about three quarters back from the front, and directly in front of the seat was a small control panel. Below that was a computer and a twelve-volt battery, and that battery was all that was needed to initiate Pandora.

Julian decided that he wanted to test the machine, but before doing so on human life (his own), he chose to use an animal. He chose a rabbit because rabbits by nature are delicate, and if a rabbit could survive, then most anything else could too. He bought one from the local pet store. It was all gray except for one white dot on the very end of its nose. He decided to name the critter Schnoz Dot. He placed Schnoz Dot in a cage and then the cage in the center of Pandora. He put all of the settings of Pandora according to the size of the machine, exactly the same as what sent the watch a little over five hours and twenty-three minutes into the future. Using a remote control, he initiated the neutron feed, creating the familiar metallic-blue bubble. But this time, it was the size of a V.W. Bug. He turned the harmonics up sharply, creating the vortex tail that shot straight forward. At that moment, the orb turned metallic black and vanished. He quickly noted that on the ground where Pandora had been were burn marks. He looked at the ceiling and saw the white paint had been charred to a color of brown and black. *Probably not the safest place to launch*, he thought. Expecting the same results, he set the timer on his phone for when Schnoz Dot should return. He waited, and when that time mark came and went, nothing happened.

* * * * *

Julian waited and waited, falling asleep occasionally, wondering what went wrong and where or even when he might have sent Pandora and Schnoz Dot. He was completely mystified. A full twenty-four hours passed, then twenty-five and twenty-six and finally twenty-seven hours and forty-two minutes had ticked by when Julian heard the electric hum. He looked up and saw the metallic black orb that quickly vanished, and the only thing that remained was Pandora, and in the cage still was Schnoz Dot.

He immediately opened the cage to check the condition of the rabbit. It seemed groggy and confused, laying a little bit on his side and stayed that way for a few minutes. Then suddenly, his little feet kicked slightly. He stood upright quickly, looking around, alert. Julian pet Schnoz on the top of his head gently, and the fuzzy, gray ball of fur seemed just fine. But to make sure, he pulled out a carrot that he had saved in his jacket pocket. He held it for the rabbit, and the little guy began to devour it.

At that moment, he decided that he would be the next one to test the time machine, but he knew he needed to enlist the help of a friend because he wasn't certain where or when he might come back or what condition he would be in. The friend he would call on, of course, would naturally be Drake Wallace.

Chapter 5

Where No Man Has Gone Before

Julian scooped up the rabbit and carried him into the living room. Sinking into his favorite recliner, he leaned back and placed the rabbit on his chest and pulled out his cell phone to call his old friend.

Before taking the call, Drake looked down at his phone to see who it was and then answered, "Well, well, well, if it isn't my favorite mad scientist. To what do I owe the pleasure of this call, Julian? I haven't talked to you in months. Which of my half-dozen phone calls are you returning?"

Julian quickly replied. "Not a damn one."

"Then what's up?"

"I need your help."

"Help with what?"

"I just sent a rabbit to where no man has gone before."

Drake laughed and said, "And where would that be? Ellen DeGeneres's bedroom?"

"Umm, no. But that was funny. Listen, here's the deal. I need your help if you've got the time. I've got something cooking that I think you'll be really interested in."

"Well, you're in luck. As it just so happens, I'm in between jobs right now. How long do you need me for?"

"I'm not sure, a week, maybe a month, maybe several months. I'll pay you too."

"That would be great. I could use the money. So do tell, what's this all about?"

"Well, do you remember when I talked to you about my idea for a Black Hole Project?"

"Yeah, you were talking about some pretty wild shit."

"It's getting wilder."

Drake's interest was piqued. "Continue."

"No, the rest of this, you're going to have to see to believe. Tomorrow morning will be just fine if you can make it."

"Sounds good. I'll pack my stuff tonight and be there first thing in the morning, probably around ten or eleven."

"That's not exactly first thing."

"It is for me. I'm a night owl."

Julian gave a sigh. "So be it. I'll see you tomorrow…morning…ish."

* * * * *

The next morning, Julian sat on the front-porch swing, sipping a cup of hot chamomile tea as he waited for Drake, and finally at about a quarter till noon, an old, beat-up F-150 white pickup truck rattled its way down the long drive. From behind the steering wheel, Drake pointed at Julian with a friendly grin, noting that Julian's hair was shoulder length. He put the truck in park, climbed out, bowed, and said loudly, "I have arrived. Your every wish is my every command."

"I wish you were on time," Julian quipped.

"Is that any way to treat your humble servant?"

"Humble servant? Not exactly, this comes with a paycheck and you're far from humble."

"Well then, for a few shillings more, I'll even pretend to be interested in whatever the hell I'm doing. By the way, what the hell am I doing?"

"Come with me. I've got something to show you in the garage."

As they made their way through the front door across the living room and then down the short hallway that led to the garage, Drake said, "So what's with the hair? I've never seen you with long hair before."

"That's because I've never had long hair before."

"How are you holding up, Julian? Are you doing okay?"

"I'm doing fine as long as I stay immersed in my work, but as soon as I take a break from it, all the memories come flooding back, and it always pushes me in the direction of my work again. As for the hair, it's not a sign that I'm falling apart really. It's just more that I don't take the time to go and get it cut. I do manage to shave and shower every day though."

They shared a moment of silence before Julian turned the knob to the garage door and pushed it open. He pointed toward the gray tarp in the center of the garage and said, "There it is. Right there."

"What is it?"

"It's my only reason for living." He walked over, pulled back the tarp, and revealed the shiny titanium-alloy contraption that he had devised and said, "I call it Pandora, and it's a result of the Black Hole Project."

Drake said, "Really?" as he took a long look at it and then looked back at Julian with a great deal of curiosity on his face and said. "Does it work?"

"Oh, it works all right, but I haven't fully figured out exactly how to control its function yet. And that's where you come in."

"Well, what do you need from me? And exactly what does this thing do?"

"Well, do you remember how I told you that the properties of the Black Hole Project might include the ability to travel time?"

Drake said, "Oh no, you gotta be shittin' me, man."

"No, I'm not."

"Seriously? Are you saying that this thing can travel time? You've tried it out?"

"Yeah, but not on myself. So far I've tried it on a watch and a rabbit. But the thing about it is that I can't tell when or how far in time forward or backward it will go. It seems to be random and I haven't yet figured out why but there has got to be a way to regulate it."

Drake took a deep breath. "You are blowing my mind. But what's my part in this? What do you want me to do?"

"Well, here's your job. I want to send myself through time, but since I don't know how long I'm going to be gone, I need someone to stay here, wait for my return, time how long I've been gone, and then check on my condition when I get back."

"You are a madman. You have lost your ever-loving mind."

"No, I haven't lost my mind, Drake. I've found it."

"Whoa, dude!" Drake exclaimed as he rubbed the back of his neck. "You know, if anyone else on planet Earth proposed this to me, I'd recommend a straight-jacket. Anyone but you, that is. So this thing really does work? When are we gonna fire this sucker up?"

Julian looked at Drake. "How about right damn now?"

"Wow. Well, there's no time like the future. Let's do it."

"Yes. But before we do, there are two things I've got to cover with you. First, I have no way of gauging how far into the future this thing will take me. Under the exact same parameters, the amount of time that it's been gone has varied greatly, the watch, five and a half hours, the rabbit, about twenty-seven hours. So you might be doing a lot of waiting around."

"Booze will help me pass the time!"

"Drake, try and focus. I've got to figure out how to make this thing work. I have to be exact about the amount of time that this thing will travel. Otherwise, it's pretty close to useless."

"Why would it be useless? I mean, what's wrong with just showing up whenever in time forward or backward?"

Julian said, "Well, what if I want to witness specific events or one specific event? It would be a matter of luck and returning home to my original time line would be highly unlikely!"

"Okay, I got you. I understand. So what's the second thing?" Julian pointed toward the burn marks on the ceiling, and Drake said, "Whoa! Time machine did that?"

"Yeah, it sure did. We've got to find another place to fire this thing up, or it's going to fire up the whole damn house."

Drake thought for a second. "Got any ideas where?"

"Well, I was thinking about using the brick platform on the side of the house near the back where we keep the grill. And check this out. I made it portable." He pulled the pins on either side of the machine which allowed him to fold it in half, and when the front and back guardrails came together, they acted as a handle.

"How much does that thing weigh?"

"About eighty-five pounds, and it'll fit nicely in most any trunk in case I need to haul it somewhere. But I'll pull the SUV around to the side of the house. You can hang out and listen to the radio until I come back, but once I'm gone, don't go anywhere till I come back. All right, man?"

"You have my word. I'll be right here."

With the time machine in tow, Julian and Drake headed off to the west side of the house toward the back where the brick platform was located. On the way, Julian explained to Drake what he would see and hear and that he wanted to test out Pandora before actually attempting to travel time. He wanted to initiate the neutron bubble for only a few seconds just to see what life was like inside the metallic blue orb.

They pulled up to the launch site, hopped out, and made their way to the back of the SUV. They unloaded

Pandora, and Julian popped it open, unfolded it, and set it up. He was standing on one side and Drake on the other. Julian looked down at the time machine, took a deep breath, then puffed his cheeks and exhaled. He looked at Drake and said, "Well, this is it, I guess. I'll be all right, right?"

Drake replied, "Rabbit lived."

"Yeah, it did."

"You'll be fine then. Give it a go."

Julian held his hands up and flicked them as if they were wet to shake them free of excess water and said, "Yes, yes, yes. I'll be fine. I'll be fine. I'll be fine." Then he slowly sat down into the seat of Pandora, looked up at Drake, and said, "I'll be fine."

"Yes, you'll be fine."

"Well then, it's the moment of truth. I'm going to crank this sucker up, and I'm going to run it for about ten to fifteen seconds and then shut it back down, and um…we'll see what happens."

Drake said, "Yep, let's do it." He pulled out his cell phone and brought up the stopwatch app in order to time the experiment.

Julian looked over the settings carefully as he had never operated the machine without a remote control before. Once satisfied, he looked up at Drake, held his finger over the start button, and said, "Here goes nothing'." He pushed the button.

The familiar electric hum began, and an instant later, the ball of metallic blue formed. Drake watched, and his jaw dropped in amazement. He noted that five seconds had ticked by and then fifteen, twenty-five, thirty-five, and finally forty-two seconds before the ball faded into nothingness.

Then Drake could see Julian once again and Julian had a smirk on his face of satisfaction and wonder.

Drake shouted, "Oh my God! That was amazing! The light show, if nothing else, was worth the price of admission. It was like looking at a controlled circular electrical storm that formed in the shape of a ball. Man, what a trip. Are you okay?"

"Yeah, I'm fine. Euphoric, if you want to know the truth. That was just amazing. It was like I was weightless, only I wasn't. It was like I was in a dream, only I was wide-awake. Everything was so surreal and comfortable. I had to shut it down quick because I wasn't familiar with the whole experience."

"What do you mean you had to shut it down quick?"

"I only went about maybe five or six seconds at the most."

"No, brother. You were in there for forty-two seconds."

"Forty-two seconds?" Julian shouted. "No, it couldn't have been."

Drake held up his cell phone and showed him. "Check it out, forty-two seconds."

Julian stood up and got off of it and then walked around the time machine, looking down at the ground the whole time and said, "Drake, it didn't just slow my perception of time. It slowed my entire metabolic pace so that time itself for me wasn't the same as it was for you, even though I never actually traveled time. That's amazing because I could swear I was only in there about five or six seconds."

Drake shook his head. "Nope. Forty-two seconds, my friend."

"Hmm. Forty-two." Julian pulled out his cell phone and brought up his own stopwatch app as well and said to Drake, "Okay, let's set them both to zero. I'm going to do this again." He sat back down. "I'm going to time this to exactly five seconds and then shut it down."

"Okay," Drake said. "Let's give it a try."

Julian got in, glanced over the settings once again, and then pushed the start button. He started his time clock as he sat inside the orb. Exactly five seconds later, he shut it down, looked up at Drake, and said, "Well?"

Drake looked at his own stopwatch. "Only thirty nine seconds this time."

Julian held up his cell phone and showed it to Drake. "Mine says five seconds, so it slowed everything down, not just my physical body but mechanics as well. I don't even know what to say."

"Well, I do. I say it's time to send your ass into the future."

Julian thought for a moment. "That's the next order of business. Now listen. This thing is going to turn metallic black, and it's going to shoot a vortex tail about three feet straight in front of me." He pointed. "And then that's when I play Houdini and disappear."

"I can't wait to see this."

"Oh, and one more thing, I'm going to put the settings on low. Hopefully I'll only be gone about twenty or thirty minutes, and like I said, don't leave me."

"I'll be here," Drake said.

Julian fired it up and pushed start. The machine created the blue bubble that then turned black and vanished.

Drake clapped his hands together and laughed out loud, staring at the empty air where Julian was just moments before. "Holy shit," he said out loud. "That did not just happen. That just happened. I just saw that. I can't believe my own eyes! Holy shit. I don't know where you went to, brother, but you sure as hell aren't here."

After a short time, the orb reappeared. Upon Julian's return, he felt slightly dizzy and sleepy, but that effect only lasted a few seconds. He looked up to find Drake standing there with his hand above his head, his fingers in the shape of a peace sign saying, "Greetings, earthling. I am Napoo from planet Nevertookapoo."

"Very funny." Julian looked down at his cell phone. "It says I've been gone eleven seconds."

Drake looked down at his. "Mine says you were gone six minutes, thirty-seven seconds."

"Damn. I could've sworn that I would've been gone about a half hour. All right, let's do this again. I'm going to put the setting slightly higher. Hopefully I'll be gone anywhere from half an hour to an hour."

"I'll be here. Mind blown again, but I'll be here."

Julian looked down and adjusted the setting slightly, looked back up at Drake and said, "Ciao." He hit the button and vanished once again.

But when he returned this time, he felt disoriented more than before, and it lasted a bit longer, about a full minute or so. He squinted his eyes and noticed that it was getting dark outside. He looked around and saw that the passenger door of the SUV was open. He could see Drake's legs but couldn't see his face since the seat was in the fully reclined position.

He shouted, "Drake! Drake, wake up. Is it dusk or dawn?"

Drake sat up, groggy, and looked out in the direction of the time machine. "Well, well, well. I was wondering if this was gonna happen."

Julian immediately noticed that Drake had a short scruffy beard and immediately replied, "Oh my God. Tell me that's fake."

"Nope."

"How long have I been gone?"

Drake looked at him and said, "Twenty-three days."

Chapter 6

Gray, From Time to Time

"Oh my God!" Julian said with a gasp. He turned his head and looked into the distance as though he could see no farther than arm's length, mouth slightly open, and his face with an expression of a man with a mathematical equation that he couldn't quite understand.

And then he said in a low, surrendering voice, "We're done for the day." He looked back again at Drake and said, "Or should I say, we're done for the month."

"Um, yeah." Drake nodded his head. "I'm ready to punch the clock. You might be fresh as a daisy, but I've been staring down some pretty serious overtime. Plus, I'm starved. Let's get something to eat."

"Well, let's get you something to eat. My lunch from a few weeks ago has only had an hour to digest. I'm okay."

They packed up the time machine and headed back inside the house. On the way, Drake asked, "So how was your journey? What was it like in there traveling through time?"

"It was like being inside of an electric fish bowl! The neutrons spinning around me gave the visual sensation that I was falling, but my body felt like it was floating. It was so wild! All the hair on my body was raised, causing my skin to tingle, and it felt like all of my movements were slow and dreamlike. All of it was just so much for my senses to take in. The sound was like static ringing in my ears, like when you're in a quiet place right after a loud rock concert. But for me, it only lasted moments. Then the bubble faded, and I felt drunk and disoriented like I was underwater but couldn't fully come to the surface. It felt that way for a minute or two, and then in an instant, I felt normal, and that's when I saw your bearded face!"

Drake said, "Sweet mother of Jesus! That must have been some ride. Sounds like something right out of *Doctor Who*. Maybe you should've made Pandora in the shape of a phone booth!"

Julian chuckled and replied, "Or a carnival ride!"

Once inside the house, Drake made his way straight for the kitchen to eat anything he could find, making his way through the refrigerator and washing it all down with the malt liquors he had bought the previous day. Julian, on the other hand, went straight to the reclining chair but not to recline. He sat on the edge of the chair with his elbows on his knees. Though his brain knew that it was dark outside, his body was still set on early afternoon. He thought to himself, *I'm as alert as I should be for the time of day I just came from, but why was I so out of it when I first came back? I guess I could call that time lag.*

About ten minutes later, Drake emerged from the kitchen, licking his fingers and pounding back the last of the malt liquor, and said to Julian, "I'm gonna crash right here on your couch if you don't mind. I just want to sleep somewhere that I don't have to flip a lever in order to lay back."

"No, of course not, go right ahead. And in fact, down the hallway there in the closet just above the towels are blankets. Help yourself."

"Thanks. It got a little old sleeping in the SUV." He made his way down the hallway and raised his voice loud enough for Julian to hear as he opened the closet door and rummaged for a blanket. "Are you okay, man?"

"Yeah, of course, I am. I'm frustrated, but I'm fine. Why? Don't I seem fine?"

Drake grabbed a light-brown blanket, closed the closet door, and said, "I don't know, man. You're missing twenty-three days of your life. I mean, if that were me, I'd be pretty freaked out."

Julian thought for a moment. "Well, no, actually. I'm not missing any days at all."

"How's that?"

"Well, assuming that I die of natural causes, whenever my death would be, I'm just going to die twenty-three days later than I would have. I'm only trading one set of twenty-three days for another. And as a matter of fact, as I sit here right now, I'm actually twenty-three days younger than I would have been. You're the one that aged, not me."

Drake plopped down on the couch, flat on his back. "Julian, you're so Julian. You see everything from a different angle." He pulled the blanket over himself and said, "I guess you're right though. I'm beat, man. I'm just gonna fade off to sleep if you don't mind."

"Go right ahead." And before he knew it, Drake very quickly drifted off. Julian was alone once again.

One hour led into the next, and Julian was unable to shut down his mind and sleep. He wandered upstairs into his bedroom to watch TV and then after a bit, went back downstairs into the kitchen for a bite to eat. Then he found himself in the living room again where he paced back and forth, humorously keeping rhythm with the sound of Drake's snoring. And then he went back up to his bedroom to check his emails. As he sat at his desk, he looked over and noticed that the glow of the moonlight shining in the windows was very bright. He walked over to the window and noticed that the duck pond and backyard area was brighter than he had ever seen it before at night.

Curious, he stepped outside of his bedroom and went down the hall, looking through the windows on the opposite side of the house. He saw that the moonlight was shining directly in through the windows from both sides of the house. He went downstairs to the front door and stepped outside to take a look at the moon for himself.

What he saw was not the moon or any other heavenly body. It was a huge triangular-shaped object, so large that it made the house look like a shed by comparison. It was hovering, silent and motionless. Fear and disbelief collided as his mind was overloaded by the sight that he beheld. He felt as though he had swallowed his own throat as he managed to speak three words, "Oh my God!" His survival instincts kicked in, and he scrambled back into the house to wake Drake. He slammed the door behind him and shot across the living room shouting, "Drake! Drake, wake up! Drake, wake up!" He shook his friend by the shoulders repeating, "Drake, wake up, man! Wake up!"

At that moment, he heard a voice but not with his ears. It seemed as though the sound came from inside his head but not generated by his thoughts or his mind, a calm, higher-than-average pitch, monotone voice said, "Be still." Julian turned his head sharply to the right but not to scan the room. It was as though his eyes knew precisely from where the voice had emanated. What his sight fell upon sent a bone-chilling shock through his body that pierced his soul and shook him to the very core of his being.

His stomach was in a tingling knot. And just as it was earlier, the hairs of his body raised as if they were charged by electric skin. He stood there, motionless, paralyzed by fear. What stood before him was a thin, wiry creature about four and a half feet tall with a large cranium and large, solid-black eyes about three times the size of the average human eye. It had long arms that hung nearly to the knees with three fingers and one opposing thumb and pasty skin that by the majority of eyewitness accounts of alien encounters would only be described as a typical Gray. Its nostrils were flat against the surface of its face with no protruding nose. Its mouth never opened, and its lips never moved as it spoke inside the mind of Julian once again, saying, "Be not afraid. Harm will not find you."

Julian's hand dangled down, tapping Drake on the shoulder as he said in a low whisper, "Come on. Come on. Come on, man, come on."

The being then said, "You will not be able to awaken him. We have deepened the sleep of that one."

With a laser-like focus in his eyes, Julian continued to stare at the creature and thought to himself, *No harm, huh? How do I know you're not going to kill me?*

But what Julian didn't realize was that the creature could hear his thoughts and replied, "If your death was our purpose, you would have never seen or heard us." Julian wondered if that response was just a coincidence, but the creature responded *no*.

Then he thought, *You can read my mind?*

And it answered *yes*. And Julian's level of fascination deepened even further.

And Julian then communicated with only his thoughts silently. *How much of my mind can you read?*

And it replied, "All."

And then he thought, *If you can read my thoughts, then what is my only reason for living?*

It replied, "Pandora."

Is that why you're here?

Again it replied, "Yes."

Are you here to take Pandora?

"If we came here to take Pandora, you would have never seen or heard us."

Julian went back to communicating verbally as he said in a surrendering tone, "I don't understand."

It said, "We will show you."

"You keep saying *we*. Are the rest of you up there?"

"Yes. And we will join them now." At that moment, it seemed as though the entire room, Drake and all, down to its very last molecule, dissolved before his eyes and then re-formed. Julian knew in his heart that it was not an illusion and that now he was aboard the alien craft. What he noted first was that there was metallic-gray flooring beneath his feet and the same type of material over his head, but it seemed as though the craft had no walls. He could see very clearly the darkened landscape and horizon in all 360 degrees.

At various points around him from some thirty to forty feet away were what seemed to be table-like control panels with no wires or visible means of support but rather stationary and operated by several other creatures that were very similar to the first. They showed no curiosity or interest that he was aboard. One of them walked from one side of the room to the other and looked down at the control panel that was being operated by yet another of these creatures. They both looked up at each other and nodded slightly. The first one walked back to where it came from.

Julian looked at the creature who had appeared in his house. "Are they communicating with each other?"

It said *yes*.

"Can they read my mind also?"

"Yes."

"Why can't I hear what they're thinking?"

The creature said, "If and when they speak to you, you will hear them."

Julian looked back in the direction of the third alien, arched his eyebrows, and said with a hint of sarcasm, "Well, that's fair… I guess."

And then the first creature, never wavering from his deadpan, emotionless way of communicating, looked at Julian and said, "Humor."

Julian found that it was difficult to control what he was thinking as he thought to himself, *I'll bet humor isn't something that happens very often around here.*

The being responded, "Humor has no sustained purpose."

Julian said, "Sorry. It comforts me when I'm nervous."

In response to Julian's anxiety, the being turned to him and extended his right arm toward Julian's face with his three fingers spread wide and pointing upward and its opposing thumb pointing downward. In the center of its hand, Julian could see a gold-colored pyramid with a capstone that was a human eye, just the same as you would find on the back of a dollar bill. Like a three dimensional hologram, it projected several inches from the center of its palm and then began to glow gold and then flickered. When it did, the warm golden glow shot instantly through Julian's body, first through his eyes, then his head, down his neck, into his arms, legs, and feet.

It was over in an instant, but when it was, Julian felt calm and blissful, as though he were in the company of close friends. Julian touched his face with both hands, dragged them slowly down to his chest and stomach. He held his arms out in front of him with hands open, examining each limb as though he was searching to identify what just overcame him.

He said to the being, "That was incredible. I've never felt so at peace."

The pyramid retracted back into the palm of the being's hand as it lowered its arm, and Julian said, "This feels amazing. How long will this last?"

The being simply replied, "As long as you are in our presence, it will serve you."

Julian now felt comfortable enough to speak freely and ask the being anything. The first question he had was, "That symbol that came out of your hand, you know I know what it is, but what does it mean for you?"

The being responded, "It's a marker, an index file that pertains to your race. It's the symbol we use when we communicate about Earth or its inhabitants."

"Why is it on our money?"

The being simply responded, "We sometimes leave impressions on the special ones that we contact, George Washington, Gandhi, Buddha, Tutankhamen, and many more."

Julian sharpened his tone and said, "You influenced the direction of our history and thereby changed the course of mankind?"

"The flow of mankind will continue where it will. We simply help it to evolve."

Julian looked at the being. "If that's so, then why get involved? Why not just let mankind evolve on its own?"

"The evolution of the majority of sentient beings leads to extinction by their own hands, and if extinction is avoided, then the evolution of that species will continue and eventually join in the chorus of universal life."

Julian was aghast by the possibilities. "You mean, someday we will travel and live among intelligent life from all over the galaxy?"

It answered, "That is our hope and our intention."

Julian's mind was spinning. "You can't be suggesting that I'm a special one because I'm not. I'm no George Washington. I'm no King Tut or any of the others. I have no impact on mankind."

"The majority of the special ones that we contact fail to make an impact. They either succeed, or they do not. They have only one chance to make a difference."

"Well, assuming that I take on this task, which I have not yet, what is my role? What is my purpose? What am I supposed to change or influence?"

"Your potential purpose cannot be revealed to you because with certainty, it would alter the outcome."

"The outcome of what." Julian still had so many questions. "How am I supposed to know what to do if I don't even know what my purpose is?"

It responded, "You will know by instinct, by who you are, your personality, your knowledge, your background. These are the reasons why you were chosen."

Julian placed his hands in a position of prayer over his nose and mouth as his eyes darted from left to right several times in an effort to make sense of all he was taking in. He took a quick breath, pulled his hands away from his face, and with his palms facing upward, said, "Okay, let's back up a bit. How did you even know about Pandora or even how to find me to begin with?"

"You are one of a handful who has discovered the principles of time travel and only the second to achieve it. But none of you understand all of the mechanics that are involved in time travel itself. To do so, one must leave one's own dimension at one point and then reenter at another, and when that is achieved, it creates a rift in the time-space continuum of that particular dimension, and our sensors were able to pick that up. And when they did, it took only moments to find you and research the content of your mind. And in doing so, we discovered that you were a viable point of contact."

Julian replied, "Okay, so that explains how you found me, but what about George Washington and Gandhi? I mean, they didn't have a time machine that could cause a rift. How did you find them?"

"That we found you was largely coincidental. It was a matter of being in the right place at the right time. But the thoughts generated by the masses eventually lead us to a handful of others like Thomas Edison, Edgar Cayce, Nikolai Tesla, and others."

"That's a pretty powerful list of names," Julian responded.

It replied, "I've only mentioned a few of the names that you would recognize, but there are many more that have played a part that you would never know and even more who have played a part and never even knew that they did."

"That's an awful lot for the mind to digest in a single sitting. So where does my journey begin, and what does Pandora have to do with all of this?"

The being replied, "It is time that we now begin." As the other two aliens looked back at the one, all three nodded simultaneously. The other two then turned their attention back to their control panels. The ceiling became as transparent as the walls, and though they were still inside the alien craft, it now appeared as though they were on top of it.

Julian looked upward toward the galaxy in wonderment when suddenly every star above shot in the same direction across the night sky. Julian noticed immediately that the vessel was as steady as a rock, as if it were not moving. The stillness of the craft gave him the sensation that the Earth and the heavens were moving in unison, as if the vessel was in a fixed position when in fact, it was the starship that was in motion.

Then all of the stars disappeared as the vessel moved into daylight. It felt strange to Julian that there was no physical sensation of movement even as the craft slowed and then stopped. He could feel nothing. For him, it was like standing on top of a building and watching a movie on a giant screen. He looked around in every direction and saw plush, green landscape as far as the eye could see. There were also a few small farms and crops. Julian asked, "Where are we?"

And it responded, "We are above the land that you call England."

He said in humbled disbelief, "Oh my God. England? That entire trip only took about ten or fifteen seconds."

"13.2 seconds. We have to travel slowly when inside an atmosphere."

Slowly? Julian thought. *We must seem like little more than primates in your eyes.* The being said nothing but guided Julian toward the starboard side of the ship and pointed downward toward the west. Julian, looking down, could see in the farmer's field below, perfectly formed interlocking circles that were weaved into the wheat fields. He looked at the alien and said, "Crop circles? You use these to determine where you're located?"

"No," it replied. "Crop circles only last a few days. We understand the geography of Earth very well. We don't use them to determine where we are but rather when we are."

"So you use them to pinpoint time travel, not navigation? Well, your time travel device is obviously far more advanced than mine, so what interest could you possibly have in Pandora, and exactly what part of England are we located right now?"

It replied, "Amesbury, Wiltshire."

Julian exhaled with a deepened look of curiosity and said, "Stonehenge?"

It replied, "Yes, Stonehenge," as it once again pointed downward but this time toward the south.

Julian could see in the overgrown, grassy fields below that it was in fact the structure known as Stonehenge. And Julian asked, "Why did your race build Stonehenge? What purpose did it serve, and why did you abandon it?"

The being explained, "We did not construct Stonehenge. It was built by humans."

Julian said, "Stonehenge is six thousand or seven thousand years old. How could prehistoric man possibly have the knowledge or the ability to build such a massive and complex structure? Those stones weigh tens of thousands of pounds and came from far away!"

"It was not built by humans from your past. It was built by humans from your future."

"Our future?"

"You see, we don't think of your people as primates because we know what the human race eventually becomes because of our guidance."

Julian was amazed. "An elder race that's nurturing an adolescent one. So why did they build this?"

"One of their crafts that traveled time and space malfunctioned and became stranded near here. They used their antigravitational technology to cut and transport these stones and then used their propulsion systems to provide the energy necessary to create a portal that would return them to their timeline. It took them a total of 337 days to complete."

And Julian said, "337? Again with 337?"

"You see, Julian, time itself is an illusion, and the number 337 is simply an echo that has been generated by a pivotal moment in your life."

"Okay then," Julian said, "let's get down to brass tacks. What is my pivotal moment?"

It said, "That moment will reveal itself."

"Okay, I'll leave it alone, but what else can you help me to understand?"

"As I told you before, in order to travel time, one must leave his own dimension and reenter at another point. But what you don't understand is that there are ebbs and flows in every timeline, and one never understands or experiences it because they are also a part of that ebb and flow. So when time moves faster or slower, it is measured exactly the same because you are within the exact same dimension of that time current. But once you leave, then you are outside of that ebb and flow. You're outside of those currents, and therefore to be able to predict the exact point of reentry for the desired arrival time is sporadic at best.

"It's why we use crop circles so that we can measure the ebbs and flows of your time dimension throughout the history of mankind. The crop circles give us exact readings of your timelines throughout the world interdimensionally, not just the location on earth but how fast or slow the currents of time run at each of those points that pertain to your planet. And from that data, it's easy to program exactly when we enter and exit according to location. It would take two hundred to three hundred more years for your people to advance this technology, but we are giving it to you now so that you have one chance to make a difference."

"But why only one chance if we can go back and forth through history? Why not more chances?"

It said, "Because a singular timeline within a dimension is stable, but multiple chances create multiple timelines within a single dimension and therefore cannot conclude as a singular outcome."

"So you're saying that I can travel freely in and out of time and even change something, but if I go back to change that one thing a second time, it would create some sort of paradox?"

"Not a paradox but a time loop for that second attempt. That second creation of a timeline within that dimension would simply repeat and go nowhere. So it's not by our decree that only one chance is given. It's that only one chance is possible."

"But doesn't traveling time itself change what would have been?"

The being said, "The course of time ebbs and flows just as a river does. But like a river, if you cast a stone into it, that river is changed forever. But how the river flows remains the same. So does the flow of time. The time-space continuum is not as delicate as mankind at this point perceives it to be.

"All that you need for Pandora is this." The being held out a flat rectangular object that looked very similar to a remote control with a few buttons on the left and right, but in the center, there were three digital readouts. The one at the top read "future." The one in the middle read "present," and one on the bottom read "past."

"How do I install this?"

"Place it in the center console of Pandora. It will adhere by itself and connect with your system's matrix. After that, you simply set the timeline for the past or the future that you wish to travel to, and it will do all the rest."

"This is priceless. This changes everything. I can't express to you how much this means to me."

"We understand how much this means to you."

Julian's eyes welled up, and his lips quivered as he asked with deep emotion and in a pleading fashion, "Can I use this to save Rebecca?"

"You can if you choose to be selfish, and if you do, you will benefit, but many more will continue to suffer."

Julian stared straight forward for a moment with a look of disgust on his face and then said, "This is cruel. Why even give this to me? Why tempt me like this? When I first invented the time machine, I figured that I could save her and that I could change anything from the past. But now knowing I can only choose one thing but that I can't choose Rebecca means that I'm just allowing her to die all over again. It's cruel." Julian looked at the being for mercy.

"It's your choice, Julian. You have free will, and we know the content of your character and the likelihood that the decision you make will be the right one."

Julian took a deep breath. "And this decision has to remain a mystery to me, or it could change the outcome. I was better off before when I had no power to change a thing."

It answered, "Those who play it safe never play a part, never make a difference, and never have the ability to impact the world."

That old, familiar feeling of numbness came over Julian, and he felt as though his body was robbed of energy. "Dust in the wind," he said. "I had a glimmer of hope. But my wife, my mother, myself, we're all just dust in the wind."

He looked down toward Stonehenge and said, "Even the people who built that, even though they haven't been born yet, they suffer the same fate as all of the rest of us." He looked down again and noticed something, saying, "There are roads that go right by Stonehenge. Where are they?"

"Those roads have not been constructed yet."

"Oh," Julian said with a wow, "what year are we in?"

"The year now is 1674."

Julian looked back out over the landscape at the farmlands again and said, "All the people that live here, all of these people, they're all dead in my time, long gone."

It said, "At the time of your life, there will have been over one hundred billion people who lived and died on your planet. But in each of their time periods, they are all alive and well. As I said before, the passage of time is an illusion. Look down at the crop circles once again."

And when he did, the crop circle had changed.

"The year now is 1822," The crop circle changed again. It said, "The year now is 1912." And then roads appeared as it said, "The year now is 1963." Another change. "The year now is 1996." And it changed again. "The year now is 2009."

Julian asked, "Why here? Why do you make so many crop circles here?"

"The currents of time that flow through here are very rapid. It's why the people from your future chose to build Stonehenge here to give themselves the best chance possible of returning to their own time, even though the stones that they had to quarry were hundreds of miles away."

Julian was blown away by his ancient-history lesson of the future from his alien instructor and said, "I've always thought of myself as an intelligent individual, but right now, I've never felt so small." After a few seconds of pondering, he said, "I wanted to save her because otherwise I would never get over her. And it looks as though now I never will." Julian thought to himself, *God, why have you made my road so difficult to travel?*

The being said, "Those who have been given the broadest shoulders bear the heaviest load."

Julian smirked and said, "I keep forgetting you can hear my thoughts." He continued, "The burden of my choice is to preserve the grim fate of the ones that I love so dearly in exchange for the end of suffering for the many that I will never even know." Julian continued, "I can't guarantee you that I'll make the right choice, you must know that. So how can you know that I will?"

It responded, "We don't!"

* * * * *

In the time frame where they came to rest, it was just before the dawn over Stonehenge in 2009. Julian's heart was heavy, and his emotions were depleted. He looked upward toward the sky, and gazing at all the stars, he said to the being, "Is there an end to the universe?"

"Yes, there's an end to *this* universe."

"This universe, there's more than one, isn't there? I knew it. How many are there?"

And the being said, "In all the times of our travel, we have not yet found an end."

"I knew it! I damn sure knew it. Ha to all who said nae!"

Julian continued to stare upward for what seemed like a full minute, but in reality, it was only about five or ten seconds, his mind trying in vain to grasp the concept of infinity. He looked back at the creature and said, "I just got a lot smaller. My fears, my dreams, my existence itself in the grand scheme of things, these are so insignificant and so very, very small." He placed his hands over his eyes and rubbed gently and then brushed his hands through his long hair and said, "I'm very tired now."

The being said, "Yes, it's time for you to sleep." It extended its arm and hand. The pyramid projected from its palm once again. The next thing Julian knew, he was waking up in his bed back at his home.

Chapter 7

Spanky

At first, as Julian lay there in bed, he looked around the room quickly but cautiously. He threw the covers off of himself as he sat up and said, "No, no, no. That couldn't have been a dream. That was just too real. That could not have been a dream." He got out of bed and went to the window. Looking out, he could see no curious lights shining outside. He shot out of his bedroom and down the hallway, looking through the windows on both sides of the house, and still he saw no curious lights. He flew down the stairs and saw Drake, still asleep on the couch. Everything was exactly the same. This time he made no effort to awaken Drake. Julian pulled his cell phone from his pocket to find that only three minutes had gone by since the time he thought he had encountered the alien. But he also realized he felt fully rested even though he had only been asleep for three minutes. He darted toward the door that led to the garage in order to check on Pandora. As he opened it, the sight of the old, gray tarp slowed his pace. Making his way over, he pulled the tarp back to find Pandora undisturbed and thought to himself, *That could not have been a dream. It just couldn't have been, especially since I was asleep for only three minutes. That's just too much to dream in three minutes.*

He made his way back in through the living room and then out the front door. He looked up at the star-riddled sky in search of any evidence of an alien craft, if for no other reason than to prove to himself that he was not crazy. But he saw nothing out of the ordinary and thought that maybe it actually was just a dream. *Maybe my preoccupation with why the time machine wasn't functioning as I anticipated was the reason. That and twenty-three days of time travel scrambled my brain a bit. But then why do I feel so awake? If I encountered an alien or not, it was still only three minutes, unless the dream itself provided an adrenaline rush that for the moment is making me feel like I'm rested.*

Julian decided to go back up to his bedroom to try and get some sleep. He figured that if it was only an adrenaline rush, then in no time, he would be able to drift off. As he made his way up the stairs, he mumbled to himself, "Dream, dream, dream. Yep, dream." He sat down on the bed and said once more, "Yeah, had to be a dream, had to be a dream. Had to have been." He laid back and pulled the sheets over himself, rolled over toward his nightstand to check that his alarm was turned on, and then he saw it. There on the nightstand was the remote control-shaped object with three digital readouts in the middle.

In a low-toned, pleasantly surprised voice, he said, "There you are, you little rascal. No dream. No dream 'cause here you are!" He grinned like the Cheshire Cat, and with a chuckle, he picked it up, rolled back onto the bed, and said, "No dream at all 'cause here you are right in my hands, you little rascal! I'm going to name you Spanky." Suddenly energized, he sprang from his bed and said, "No need for sleep 'cause I ain't sleepy! Come on, Spanky. Let's go for a ride."

With a newfound spring in his step, he made his way back down the hall, down the stairs, and past the still-snoring Drake. He held the device in his right hand, pointed at it with his left, and said to Drake, "Alfalfa, meet Spanky."

Once inside the garage, he yanked the gray tarp off of Pandora and sat down, holding the device out from his body in both hands and said, "Now somehow, you're supposed to adhere to the console all by yourself." Assuming that the device was magnetic, Julian extended it toward the center of the console. When metal touched metal, the surrounding area of the console turned to a liquid metal. It didn't spill downward but rather stayed in place. Julian let go of the device immediately, and it sank in until the surface of the device was even with the surface of the console. Then the liquid metal turned solid once again as though it had been built in and was there all along.

With fascination, he said, "Whoa," as he tapped his finger around the surface of the console that had just been liquid. He pondered. "Okay, that was different. Yah, don't see that sort of thing every day. But after the night I've had, not a big shock either. And I'm going to assume that you're all hooked up because it doesn't look like you're going anywhere anytime soon." And when he said that, all three of the digital panels lit up in glowing red simultaneously, day, month, and year, each set at zero. "Well, hello there, Spanky. Looks like you've made yourself right at home."

Julian wasted no time folding Pandora in half and hauling it out to the platform in the side yard where they had launched from before, and along the way, he began talking to himself saying, "I'm keeping my promise, Rebecca. My first stop is August 28th two years ago. And if I remember correctly, we were on the back patio an hour or so before dusk." As he began to unfold Pandora in the side yard, he paused and thought to himself, *No wait. I can't do this here. I can't run the risk of Rebecca seeing two of me or even me seeing myself.*

So he went off into the woods where he knew that there was a clearing of a natural, rocky, mostly gravel area where he could launch from. He was about fifty or sixty yards from the house with the machine set up.

He sat down and got ready to launch. He took a deep breath, looked at Spanky on the control panel, and said to himself, "This is going to work, right? I mean, they're aliens. They know what they're doing, right?" He punched in August 28th two years prior and set the clock at 7:00 p.m. His finger hovered over the start button, and then he pulled it back. He reached toward the start button a second time and pulled it back again. He said to himself aloud, "Let's see. If Drake were here, he'd say, 'No time like the past.' Okay, so I'm just going to do it then," and then he leaned forward, pressed the button...and vanished.

* * * *

When he and the machine reappeared, Julian once again felt a combination of groggy and dizzy that lasted only for a minute or two. He was quickly able to dismiss the feeling and thought to himself, *I guess this is the usual when it comes to time travel for the contraption that I've built because it certainly didn't feel this way aboard the alien ship.*

He looked around, and it was daylight. He could tell by the hue of the sun that it had to be early evening. So the time of day he set on the time machine appeared to be correct. *But was the date correct? How can I know exactly?* he thought to himself. *I guess I could go out and buy a newspaper to make sure I'm on the right date.* He looked down at Spanky and saw that the digital read-outs for both past and present each read, "August 28th of the same year." *It says so, so I guess it is so.* And with that, he made his way toward the house. He figured either he or Rebecca was going to emerge any time now.

As he approached the pond area near the edge of the woods, he got down on his hands and knees and crawled through the brush. He settled in, taking a vantage point between the leaves and the branches where he had a clear view of the dock and patio area. He waited for about fifteen more minutes and then saw himself walk out of the house. It was bizarre and surreal. He felt as though he was outside of himself. It was strange, like a movie, but instead, was real life.

Julian of the past was carrying two wine glasses, a bottle opener, and a bottle of Merlot, all of which he placed on the patio table next to the round loaf of bread, precisely as he had remembered himself doing before. He returned to the kitchen, and less than a minute later, the patio door reopened. He froze as he watched them walk out onto the patio, first Rebecca and then him. The emotional intensity that gripped his body was far more powerful than he had mentally prepared himself for.

It had been nearly a year and a half since he had last seen her, and the reservoir of tears for his beloved wife that he had drawn from so many times in the past was overflowing once again. He was on his knees when he placed his hands on the ground in front of him, dropping his head down as his love for her dripped from his eyes. When he looked back up again, his face was beet red. His mouth was open, and his teeth exposed. It was the expression that only comes from the gut-wrenching pain that's felt deep within the heart.

Although from the very conception of Pandora it was intended to save her, he felt that if he couldn't, then seeing her in that timeline, he would find peace, but it was extremely painful instead. Yet he couldn't leave. He couldn't take his eyes off of her…because there she was. He wanted so badly to touch her, to hold her, and to tell her how much he missed her. But this reunion could not be shared. The agony of the moment was for him and for him alone.

He watched as they sipped their wine, snuggled, and laughed, reveling in the joy of each other's company. He listened carefully. It was difficult to hear the distant conversation that they had so long ago, but he heard himself say, "Note to self, come back and visit August 28 often." He felt as though he had fulfilled his promise and that it was time to go. He couldn't stand the tearing of emotions any longer.

He whispered, "Goodbye, my sweet, precious girl. I have to go now, but here in this time you will forever be happy, safe, and well. My time goes on without you."

He took one last, long look at her as he wept, and he blew her a kiss. As he turned to crawl back out of the brush, a cramp in his leg from sitting docile for so long caused his movement to be unsteady, and he accidentally rattled the bush next to him. In a panic, he scampered toward the woods as he could hear his past self say, "What was that? It was right over there."

And he heard Rebecca say, "It was probably just a deer, my dear."

Knowing that he did not pursue himself, he felt no urgency to return to the time machine. And though the experience was bittersweet, in all, he felt it was worth it. Emotionally drained yet physically energized by his newfound freedom of passage because of Spanky, he decided that it was time to visit his father, the man that he never had the chance to know. Upon returning to the rocky opening in the woods, Julian settled into Pandora and set Spanky for a time when he was just a toddler, figuring from that point he could visit again and again with his father before he met his untimely death.

* * * * *

When he arrived, he again had to shake off the effects of time lag and refocus. As he made his way back toward the house, he noticed that trees that were once large and tall were now small and trees that he remembered as saplings at this point did not exist. As he approached, he saw the old house that he grew up in, not the two-story house, no patio dock, no lake. But instead of the rickety, run-down house, he remembered from his teenage years, at this time, the house was well kept and quaint. *This made all the difference,* he thought to himself. His mother with a husband, a man around the house to tend to things that a woman struggling to raise a child on her own would not have the time to take care of.

Since Julian had no idea where his parents would be or if they were even home, he figured it best if he circled his way out toward the road and approached the house from the driveway rather than just as a stranger who appeared out of the woods. Now all he had to do was concoct a reason for being there.

Let's see, he thought to himself. *Lost and need directions won't work because I want to visit here a number of times, which means I'll need a number of reasons. Salesman won't work for the same reason. Besides, Mom never cared for door-to-door salesmen. I guess I could say I'm new to the neighborhood and wanted someone to show me around. Hmm. That sounds kind of lame, but it's the best I've got. It'll have to do. And what should I call myself?*

Julian decided to call himself Brandon because it was the name he would have given his son, if his son had been given the chance to be born. As he approached the house, the feeling of nostalgia that had been with him for so long began to melt away. He felt as though he were walking on sacred ground. Once standing at the front door, he lingered for a moment, hesitant to ring the doorbell. He felt as nervous as he did as a young man, ringing a doorbell to greet a young lady on his very first date. He rang the doorbell, and after a few moments, the door opened. It was his mother. He was taken aback immediately by how young and vibrant she looked. He stammered, but before he had any chance to speak, she said, "Whatever it is you're selling, I don't need any. You can be on your way."

He recovered and said, "No, no, ma'am. I'm not selling anything. My name is Brandon, and I'm new to the area. I don't live too far from here."

She said, "Oh, I thought you were going to try to sell me a vacuum or a life-insurance policy or something. Well, what can I do for you, Brandon?"

"Well, I was just up at Bobba Lou's Grocery, asking around if there was anyone in the area who might know some good hunting and fishing spots and maybe even be interested in somebody to tag along with. And they said Gabriel up on Lockwood Drive might be interested because his wife spends most of her time tending to a little one. I take it that's you? So I thought I'd stop in and see if I could—"

She cut him off and said, "Well, first of all, I don't know what Bobba Lou's Grocery is all about. It's Bobba's Grocery. I know that he does have a nephew named Lou that just helps his uncle at the store. And as for my husband, yeah, his name is Gabriel, but we all call him Gabe, and so do the people at Bobba's. So how you came up with Gabriel, I don't know."

Julian's nerves were getting to him but thought quickly. "Well, I'm sorry. I guess I was trying not to be too informal."

"Well, Gabe certainly does like to be formal but not when he's hunting or fishing. My name's Carly, by the way. Would you like to come in?"

"Why, yes. Yes, I would."

She opened the door wider and stepped back to let him in, and when she did, he saw a tiny little boy standing behind her to the left. He was clinging to her dress. It was a young Julian Phillips.

He knew that he was going to see himself, but he was astonished nonetheless to be standing in front of his toddler self. He knelt down and said, "Oh my God. I really was a cute little… I mean, he really is a cute little thing," as he looked back up at his mother.

"Most two-year-olds are," she replied with a smile. "No motherly bias here though." And she laughed out loud. "Gabe," she yelled. "He's around here some-where," she said to Julian.

He looked down at his mini-me, and at the same time, his mini-me looked back up at him. They both smiled in unison as though they were twins. Their facial gestures and their reactions were identical. His mother folded her arms in amusement as she watched and said, "You know, there's something familiar about you. Something comfortable, I guess. Maybe it's your demeanor or the way my little boy is reacting to you that tells me you're an okay guy."

Julian's heart warmed. "Thank you. I can tell there's a lot of love in this house. I feel like I'm home."

"You're right about that part," she said. "There's a lot of love all right."

"Gabe," she yelled again. She continued talking to Julian. "I've got a good man, and he gave me a wonderful son. And I suppose if the marriage is good, everything else falls into place. What about you? Are you married?"

Julian looked down at the floor. "I was. She passed away."

"Oh my," she said with compassion. "I'm… I'm so sorry."

He looked back up at her and said with painful sincerity, "Me too."

Just then, they heard the back screen door open and then slam shut. Julian's father made his way to the living room through the side hallway. As he peered around the corner, he said, "Where's the fire?"

"Where were you?" Carly asked.

"I was on the side of the house stacking firewood. What's going on, and who's our guest?"

"This is Brandon. He's new around here and was looking for someone to hunt and fish with."

"Perfect. I'm going fishing next Sunday. You up for it?" Julian, in awe of his presence, replied "Um yeah, I mean yes, next Sunday sounds great."

Gabe had a soft baritone voice, the kind that would carry all the way across the room without being raised. He was tall and gentle in nature. With a manly Midwest look, he carried himself with a calm confidence. Julian was speechless. For him, seeing his father was like seeing a famous rock star that never took the stage.

His father held out his hand and said, "Hi, I'm Gabe."

Julian, for a few seconds, was awkwardly motionless as his eyes were in wonderment at the sight of his father, and then he raised his hand to shake, saying, "I'm Brandon." On the outside, he was cordial and calm, but on the inside, he was dying. He wanted to yell at the top of his lungs, "I'm your son! I'm your son!"

A single tear rolled from his eye as Gabe looked at him a little closer and said, "Are you all right?"

Julian said, "Yeah," as he scrambled for an excuse. "I just got some, some hot pepper juice in my eye earlier. I guess it's still rolling around in there."

"Hey, you like your food spicy too, huh? What kind of pepper was it?"

Julian scrambled once again and just blurted out, "Uh, uh, a Scotch bonnet."

Gabe laughed. "Ha! That's my favorite pepper too. Looks like you and I have more in common than we know. Most people can't stand a pepper that hot. It's rare I find someone who does. Funny." Gabe continued, "Well, like I said, I'm going fishing next Sunday. I like to get out there at the crack of dawn, so if you can get here about, I don't know, five thirty or so, does that work for you?"

Julian smiled. "Yeah, that works for me just fine. I'll be here."

Carly chimed in. "What's it going to be, Gabe, politics or fishing? You're not going to have enough time for both."

Gabe turned to look at his wife and said, "Guess what, honey. I've made an executive decision. I'm going to run for town council after all! But I'll still fish here and there," as he smiled and then continued. "Now what I've got to do, my darling, is scramble up some support, maybe get some volunteers. Brandon here might even be interested in helping me out. And I've got to get posters and bumper stickers made up. And, uh, I was thinking about a slogan. How about 'Honest Gabe'?"

"You are such a dork," she said with a chuckle. "But hey, it worked for Lincoln!"

At that, Julian decided he'd best be on his way, though he wanted to stay. He figured it was better to ease into their lives a little at a time rather than run the risk of being shut out completely. He smiled at them and said, "I'll be more than happy to help with the campaign. And I'll see you next Sunday at around five thirty. But I've got to get going." He shook hands with Carly and Gabe, (mom and dad) and then looked down at his toddler self, patting him on the head and saying, "I don't need to tell you to be a good boy. I know that you are."

They bid him farewell and saw him to the door. As Julian walked out, he did not look back when he said good-bye for fear that they would see the tears welling up in his eyes. As he made his way down the old cobblestone driveway toward the road, before reentering the woods to find the time machine, he decided it was best if he went back to his own timeline to regroup, get some rest, and contemplate his next move.

He set Spanky for ten minutes after the original point that he left his timeline so he would not see himself leaving. He figured that he would have about two hours of sleep, which was all he really needed before Drake would likely wake up. Once he arrived back in his own timeline, he folded Pandora in half and walked through the now more familiar woods that he knew so well. He went into the garage, threw the tarp over the time machine, and then headed in the house. He made his way past the yet still-snoring Drake and up the stairs into his room for some much needed shut-eye.

* * * * *

The next morning when Julian woke, his head was buzzing with thoughts of what to do next, the possibilities and what-ifs. And then there was the whole issue of, *How do I explain to Drake that I took a ride with aliens? Or should I even bother to tell him at all? And if I do tell him, would he believe me?* And then he thought, *Well, I do have Spanky to back up my story, I suppose.* Either way, he hadn't eaten in a while and was hungry and figured he could get Drake up to speed on everything over eggs and pancakes down at the local diner. Plus, he knew that they served Drake's favorite morning meal—Bloody Mary.

It was an old-fashioned style of diner—chrome-lined breakfast bar stools and countertops. The walls were painted white and yellow, and the decor was classic photographs of Marilyn Monroe, Marlon Brando, Humphrey Bogart, Elvis Presley, and the like. Fifties music played from the replica jukebox over in the corner. Julian and Drake sat at the last window booth to the left as you entered the diner.

After a lengthy discussion, dissertation, and an explanation of what happened the night before, Julian concluded by saying, "And if you don't believe me, I'll show you the device itself. It's mounted literally inside the metal of the console on the time machine."

Drake stared at him for a moment, absorbing the story. "Yeah, I'd like to see that. That doesn't mean that I don't believe you, but nothing that comes out of your mouth should surprise me anymore. It sure is a wild-ass story, but I believe you. You've never thrown around bullshit, especially something as way out as this. So what's your plan?" Drake continued, "Where you gonna go from here?"

"Well, I figured the best thing I could do is to have an overview. If I go about a hundred years into the future, maybe I can look back and review where my life went and the events that happened in history up to that point and see if I can locate anything that I'm supposed to latch onto to make a difference about. Anyway, here's what I'm thinking. I should launch from Bobba Lou's in the far back parking lot."

"Why's that?"

"So I won't be seen, duh!"

"No, I mean why Bobba Lou's? Why not from your house?"

"Oh, right. Well, see, the building itself that's now Bobba Lou's was once a feed-and-grain store a bazillion years ago, and after that, it became a restaurant and bar. Some of the local lawmakers back then loved the place and decided to declare it a landmark to be preserved into perpetuity. So in a hundred years, it should still be there…maybe…hopefully…well, a much better chance than my house anyway."

"Okay, yeah. That makes perfect sense."

"So here's what I'm also thinking. When I take off from behind Bobba Lou's, it doesn't matter what time I leave because all I have to do is make sure the coast is clear, but returning, I think I'm gonna have to make sure I come back around five o'clock in the morning. That way, there's nobody there, and I'll have no chance of running into myself leaving. And it's also important, I think, if I set the time machine for the future exactly one hundred years and then my return trip for five o'clock in the morning on the same date. That way, if I run into any trouble when I arrive in the future, all I have to do is press the button a second time, and *bam*, I'm right back here at five a.m."

Julian was feeling wide-eyed from the unending possibilities and continued saying, "I don't mean to go on, but finding a meaningful way of impacting the world seems a little bit far-fetched, even with a time machine. I mean, think about it. We're in the middle of another Gulf War. Let's say I wanted to change that. How would I go about it? How could I make any difference there? Just because I have a time machine doesn't change the fact that I'm only one man. And if I never find the reason, if I never find the *it* that I'm supposed to change, well then, I'm going to have the most wild-ass bucket list anybody's ever conceived. I'm going to see the 'Sermon on the Mount,' watch Babe Ruth hit a homerun. I'm gonna check out the Beatles in concert and even go to the very first Super Bowl. It won't be hard to get a ticket for that one. It's the only Super Bowl that didn't sell out. And do you know what the best part is?"

An inspired Drake said, "What's that?"

"I'll get to hang out with my old man. We'll go fishing for walleye and trout, hunt for deer and wild pigs, and while we're doing all of that, we're going to talk. I'll find out his likes and dislikes, his views on the world, his thoughts about me. And next Sunday, thirty years ago, we will be on our first father-son fishing trip! I mean, of course, it would've been ideal to have him there for me throughout my childhood, but hell, think about it, a man that's been gone from this earth for so long and yet I get the chance to know him firsthand!"

And then Julian paused. As the look of a thousand-yard stare came over his face, he said, "There's one more thing that I have to take care of, that I have to find the courage to do."

"What's that?" Drake asked.

Another long pause.

"I'm—"

And right at that moment, their waitress, Phoebe, walked up and said, "Gentlemen, I don't mean to be rude because we do appreciate your business and all, but I did drop a check for you guys about a half an hour ago. And since then, the restaurant has filled up, and there are people waiting to be seated. So if you don't mind." She gestured toward the bill.

Julian said, "Of course. Yeah, I'll take care of that right now."

She was a cute, young thing with high cheekbones, dimples, and blonde, bouncy hair. She made small talk as Julian got out his wallet and began counting money to pay. Drake stared her up and down as though she was a fresh dessert topping. She looked back at Drake with mutual admiration as the small talk between the two of them continued.

As they were leaving, all Drake could talk about were the possibilities of a new conquest. Julian felt no need or desire to pick up the conversation where it had left off, and he just continued to listen to his own thoughts as the white noise of Drake's drivel faded into the background. Once Julian returned home with Drake, he immediately began laying out a game plan for a hundred-year leap, but it was mostly speculation of the unknown.

He got out of the car and put his hands on his hips. He paused for a moment as he went over a checklist in his head, then whirled his hand in the air in front of him, and with his palm upward, he said, "Well, I just need to pack up some sandwiches into the cooler along with some sports drinks, and I'm on my way."

Drake said, "Those sandwiches aren't going to last long. What are you gonna do about money?"

"I've got a handful of gold coins from a hundred and fifteen years ago. Gold, over a long period of time, never goes down in value. Plus, coins have intrinsic value, which means when I arrive there, they'll be a hundred years older than they are now, making them even more valuable. So once I get there, a quick trip to a pawnshop should take care of my needs for money, unless they don't have pawnshops anymore and unless currency isn't the way that business is done anymore. But I guess I'll cross that bridge when I come to it, so after you, sir." He gestured toward the house and then followed in behind Drake.

Once inside the house and in the kitchen, Julian started loading up the cooler with sandwiches. Drake said, "Hey, Julian, there was one more thing that you said that you wanted to do with the time machine. I didn't catch what it was. What was it?"

Julian slowed and then stopped loading the sandwiches. He looked back at Drake and said, "That's a tough one, man. I want to go back and find out who killed my wife and my mother and make sure the son of a bitch pays forever. All I have to do is make sure the newfound evidence I bring back makes its way into the Marion County Police's hands." He turned his head back toward the refrigerator, hesitated, and then resumed loading the cooler.

Drake was still facing Julian, but his eyes were not focused on him but rather internally. And he, too, heard a voice inside his head. It said, *You can't allow him to do that*, as his still and lifeless eyes continued to stare into nothingness. A second voice inside of Drake's head responded, *There's nothing I can do about this or any of us. We didn't do this. That Drake did, the evil one.* Yet another voice came forward and said, *But we all share this body. Something has to be done with him, or we'll all suffer.* Then the first voice said, *Then let the dark one come forward. We didn't have anything to do with this. This is his mess. Let him clean it up.*

Julian looked back at Drake as he shut the refrigerator door and popped the top of the cooler lid. "That's it, buddy. Let's get going." No response from Drake. Julian snapped his fingers in front of Drake's face saying, "Yo, anybody in there?"

Drake snapped out of it and replied, "Yeah, yeah, let's get going."

So off they went out through the front door and climbed into the SUV. All the while during the trip, Julian, in an attempt to stave off his nervousness about his journey into the unknown, spoke of things relevant and irrelevant, just chattering away to try and calm his nerves. He received no response from Drake as Drake's mind was listening to the inner argument of several voices in his head. He simply gave bland responses like,

"Yeah" and "I hear you" and "Yeah, I got you on that one" and "Sure, I know what you mean."

As they drove, Drake occasionally looked over at Julian, not hearing a single word but only seeing the movements of his mouth while the conversation in his head continued. *What are you going to do? How are you going to get out of this one?* The alternate voice said, *There's a tire iron in the back. There's no other means I can use. I'll just take him by surprise. Don't you worry. All of you just shut up and let me handle this.*

They arrived at the parking lot behind Bobba Lou's a little before midnight, Julian still babbling away and Drake mostly silent. Once Julian threw the SUV into park, he hopped out of the driver's side as Drake made his way out of the passenger's side. They both met at the back bumper, and Julian looked at Drake and said, "Are you okay, man?" as he opened the hatch. "You've hardly said a word. Or are you annoyed with all of my chitter chatter?"

Then as Julian pulled Pandora out of the back hatch, Drake eyed the tire iron that was lying just beneath. Julian turned to go and set up the machine. Drake grabbed the iron and used the curved end to latch onto the back of his blue jeans. Julian looked back briefly and noticed the odd body movement of Drake but did not see the tire iron. He thought not much about it, figuring that Drake was up to some sort of prank and that he should be on his toes. Drake followed in behind as a chorus of voices in his head all clamored at once, *Do it now. Do it now. Do it now.* As he followed, he accidentally tipped his hand by saying with a loud, teeth-clenched grunt, "Silence!"

Julian had just unfolded the time machine when he snapped back a look at Drake after his comment and said, "Excuse me, grumpy pants. What the hell is your problem? You know, I know I'm being a little bit talkative, but hell, I'm about to go a hundred years into the future. Give me a break."

Drake said, "I'm just shining you on, man, trying to loosen you up a little bit. That's all."

"Yeah, well, that's not the best thing I need right now, douchebag." Julian returned to his task of setting the time on the time machine but could tell by Drake's body language that something more was up, and he was now even more cautious.

Standing next to the time machine with Drake just a few feet away, he said, "Well, I'm ready. I've got my time set for one hundred years in the future, and I've also got my return time set as well. I'll see you in about three weeks. You'll see me in about five hours." Julian turned and looked down at the time machine thinking to himself, *Maybe Drake just doesn't have enough cocktails in him and is going through a miniwithdrawal.* Either way, as he began to straddle the time machine, he could hear the rapid scuffling of feet and turned to see Drake with the tire iron in both hands, striking in a downward motion. Julian reached with his right arm across his body and grabbed Drake's wrist.

At that point, it broke the tire iron from Drake's hand, and it fell to the ground. Drake followed with a weak left-handed punch, and so did Julian, spinning around and using Drake's momentum to toss him to the pavement. "What the hell, man! Have you lost your mind?" Julian shouted. Drake regained his footing and reached for the tire iron again. Julian, realizing he couldn't allow him to get a hold of it, charged forward and tackled him backward. They were about equal in strength, and as they rolled on the pavement, they separated from the momentum of the fall. As Julian and Drake both regained their footing, Drake charged at Julian once again as Julian said, "Give it up, man. What the hell is wrong with you? Stop this."

Fists flew, and then Drake spun around and caught Julian by surprise with a right-handed punch to the temple. Julian hit the ground, smacking the back of his head on the pavement.

He lay there dizzy with his vision slightly doubled, trying to make sense of what seemed like a bad dream. "What the hell is wrong with you?" he groggily asked. Confused, weakened, and disoriented, Julian rolled to his left, placing his hand on the ground in an attempt to stand up and then another hard punch to the face from Drake, flattening Julian right back down to the pavement again.

Drake used this opportunity to gather up the tire iron and then straddled Julian's chest. Using both hands, he held the tire iron across his neck pressing down and said, "Sorry, old friend. I guess I owe you an explanation. You see, I couldn't let you go back to find out who killed your wife because you would find me there. I just couldn't let that happen."

Red faced and steeped in anger, Julian struggled to speak saying, "Why did you kill them? Why? Why me? I've done nothing to you! Why?"

"I didn't mean to. They were in the wrong place at the wrong time. I needed money. I knew you had some in the house. I didn't expect them to be home. I thought they were still in Florida with you. It was your mother's fault. She said, 'You're going to jail for this,' and there's no way in hell somebody controls me. So I did what I had to do. I grabbed what I could find, and I hit her. At that point, your wife was going to be a goner too because now she witnessed a murder. I had to dispose of her also. Damn fools they were, both of them."

Drake kept a steady pressure on Julian's throat as he grunted for air.

"Rebecca was an easy target though because she was a trusting soul. All I had to do was tell her that it was an accident and that I wouldn't harm her as long as she helped me and didn't get in my way until I left. I asked her where the garbage bags were so I could load up some valuables, and she was gullible enough to believe me. So I popped it over her head, and the rest is history. I could have just bashed her head in the way I did your mother, but I wanted her intact. I wanted a little revenge for all those times she turned me down. No one controls me, no one."

Julian, struggling, said, "You son of a bitch. You're going to burn in hell." He tried desperately to grab at Drake's throat, but Drake pressed down with the tire iron even harder.

"It isn't going to take very much pressure for me to crush your larynx and break your neck." Julian grabbed both sides of the tire iron in an attempt to relieve the pressure on his throat. Drake said, "Don't squirm too much. I'd have no problem killing you too."

Julian's voice was gurgling slightly as he strained to speak. "How could you continue to pretend to be my friend? You even went to the funeral you cold motherfucker?"

Drake continued with his white-knuckle grip pressing downward, and with a look of pure wickedness and evil on his face, he said, "Because I found out that it gets easier every time. They weren't my first kill, not even my latest. Hell, the first guy I killed was on the roadside not far from here just a few weeks before I went off to MIT. It was something I had always fantasized about. Did you ever listen to 'American Prayer'?"

Still struggling to speak, Julian said, "No!"

"You should have because if you had, you would have heard Jim Morrison mumbling on about having killed a man just to see what it was like to take a life. I told you when he was a boy, he had seen that accident, and those migrant workers, Indians, were dying on the roadside, remember? He said that one, maybe two of them entered into his mind. I had a similar experience when I was a boy. I watched a man die. His blood flowed from his eyes and from his ears as he twitched and squirmed. That image stayed with me my whole life. And when I took my first life, I could swear that part of his soul entered my mind as well and each thereafter.

"You see, it was fate, as I was thinking about doing the very same thing as I saw this stranger walking alone on the roadside. All of a sudden, the next song on the radio was an old Johnny Cash tune singing about how he shot a man in Reno just to watch him die. Hell, even the Beatles gave Charles Manson instruction in 'Helter Skelter.' I figured it was calling to me. It was fate. It had to be. It energized me, filled me with power. After that, it became a hunger.

"Once I settled into Massachusetts, I needed to feed again some unsuspecting soul and then some months later, another one and then the ever-popular Mrs. Janet Barnes. She laughed at me when I asked her out. She said she was out of my league because I was too young, like a puppy as she put it. Stupid bitch!

"After college, you thought going from job to job was a bad thing, but moving around the country like that meant the authorities weren't likely to be able to make connections. They seemed like random acts of violence rather than serial, or so I assume. Then a hooker in Cabo San Lucas and her pimp for good measure. Hell, I needed the vacation money anyway. And I'm not even sure how many in all, but they all stayed with me. They're all still inside me, and I have their allegiance."

All the while, Julian had continued to struggle as he said, "You're not sane! You're distorted! What gives you the right to take the lives of innocent people?"

"What gives me the right?" he asked back. "What gives me the *right*? All the people of the world serve me." And then he charged his right finger straight into the air as he shouted at the top of his lungs, "Because I am God!"

Julian used that moment with all of his strength to push Drake off of the top of him as he rolled out from underneath, and as Drake fell to the side, Julian shouted, "You're a madman!" They both quickly came to their feet and Drake swung hard with the tire iron. Julian blocked with his hand, but the heavy iron rod still made contact with the side of his head. Though the majority of the blow was absorbed by Julian's hand, it was still enough to knock him out. Drake, thinking that it was a full strike to the head, thought that surely he was lying there dead. He threw the tire iron down on the pavement beside Julian.

As it clanked to the ground, he said, "Good night, Felicia, and thanks for the time machine because now I can roam through all of time immune from consequences and feed my desires wherever I wish."

A few seconds later, Julian could hear the echoed, dreamlike sound of laughter as he began to come to. He opened his eyes ever so slightly to stealthily survey his surroundings. From Julian's vantage point, a view that was parallel to the ground, he could see the fuzzy image of Drake settling into the time machine. He could also hear Drake say to himself in what sounded to Julian like a slow, low-pitched, drawn-out voice, "The world is mine. I have no limits." Then he rubbed his knees before cracking his knuckles and greedily rubbing his hands together saying, "Let's see. Where to first? I guess I could go back to 1989 or '90 and buy a bunch of really cheap Intel stocks, and maybe I could use that money to buy a crap load of property before the housing bubble. And hell, I'll buy up thousands of dollars of Bitcoin at ten cents a share. The possibilities are endless."

Julian was horrified by the damage that Drake could unleash, and in a desperate attempt to prevent it, he staggered to his feet and did the best he could to charge toward Drake. Drake realized that he had no time to change the travel setting for the time destination, so he just hit the start button. The bubble formed and then vanished as Julian collapsed to the ground in the spot where the time machine had just been only an instant before. He was too late. Drake was gone. There was nothing he could do to change that.

Bloodied and beaten, he rolled over on his back and cried out, "Oh, God, please no!" He was now powerless to stop the evil that Drake would reign upon the world. Julian felt that Pandora's box had truly been opened and the fault was his own.

Chapter 8

Cold Heart

Julian sought medical attention for several broken bones in his left hand as well as a mild concussion. In the following weeks, his wounds would heal slowly, but the scar of regret would be with him forever. He knew that he could build another time machine, but it would have no worth without a device like Spanky, as the chances of running into Drake would be one in a billion. He had no way of knowing if history had already been altered or if there was chaos in the future. For all he knew, Drake himself, was Jack the Ripper. As the days passed, the desire to right the wrong was building. The feeling of urgency to clean the mess that he had made was increasing but the cloud of, how, was looming.

Three months had now gone by, and he decided to go back down to Houston and seek the advice of James

Daniel, even though he knew that it could possibly end his career with NASA, citing insanity or mental illness.

Once arriving at Daniel's office, his secretary notified him that Julian was there to see him. Rather than wait for Julian to enter, he greeted him at the door, a brief man hug and a pat on the back, and then he ushered him in saying, "It's good to see you, Julian. It's been far too long. We really miss you and need you around here. The Man on Mars project is coming along a lot slower than we had anticipated, and I know that you could make a world of difference with that, but I understand that there's a lot going on in your life, and I'd like to hear about it."

His office was made up of mainly oak cabinets and oak bookshelves as well as a desk and an old brown-leather office chair. And adorning the shelves were old knickknacks of past NASA victories and triumphs. But the miniature tributes that were on his desk were models of Apollo 13, the space shuttle *Challenger*, and the space shuttle *Columbia*. He offered Julian a seat in the chair opposite his desk while he sat down in his own. Julian, noticing the souvenirs on his desk, said, "Why do you keep the reminder of disasters on your desk alone?"

"Because those are the most important. The ones that keep us grounded are the ones that remind us of how delicate every mission and every life is." They both looked at each other understandingly and matter-of-factly. A brief pause and then James Daniel said, "What's going on, Julian? What has brought you here?"

Julian drew a deep breath and said, "Well, I'll just be blunt and lay the whole story out for you, but I have to warn you, you might just think that I'm completely nuts, and if you do, it will certainly end my career here at NASA. But I'm at a dead end. I'm all out of options. I've got nothing left to lose. And it doesn't matter to me anymore. I know that you and I speak the same language of science, so there's a chance that you'll believe me, and that's a chance I have to take. So here goes."

James Daniel listened carefully and patiently as Julian went on for over an hour, occasionally asking a question to help clarify the picture in his mind that Julian was trying to convey to him. Julian finally said, "You might think I'm lying, crazy, or both JD, and I wouldn't blame you if you do, but that's it. I've told you everything, and I don't know what else to do."

James Daniel sat back in his chair looking at Julian with curiosity and said, "No, Julian. I don't doubt you at all. I don't just think that you believe what you're saying, but I also believe that what you're saying is true. So let's take a closer look at this. If he did make it there one hundred years into the future, then you have to realize that our reality hasn't changed at all, at least not yet because the future hasn't happened yet. In other words, until one hundred years is up, he's just as good as being in limbo. He doesn't really exist, at least right now. He's outside of our dimension and cannot touch anything until he reappears."

"That's all true, James, but he's going to reappear, one hundred years are going to pass, and when he arrives, he can then travel anywhere in time that he wants to…and then what? I have no way of getting into the future to find him and stop him from traveling back through time and start changing history."

James said, "This has been at the forefront of your mind, every second, every minute of every day, hasn't it?"

Julian nodded. "Well, of course, it has."

"Well, my friend, that might be the problem. You're looking at it far too closely."

"How so?"

"Think about this. He didn't go into the past. He went into the future. The way of bridging that gap might be much more simple than you ever thought."

Julian looked at him very quizzically. "What do you mean?"

"There's a cryogenics lab out in California."

Julian sucked in a breath. "Oh my God, why didn't I think of that? I could have myself frozen."

"Yes, you could, but that's going to present a couple of very difficult obstacles because technically, you have to be dead in order to be frozen, or else, by the laws as they are written currently, it would be considered murder. So we'd have to do two different things that would potentially end my career also. One, we would have to change your identity because if you made it back safely from the future, the public, as well as the people at the cryogenics lab, would not understand how there could be two Julians, one as a living human being and the other frozen in a lab. Two, we have to find a way to make you, for all intents and purposes, appear to be dead.

"I can work on both of these on my end. The making you appear to be dead part is the easier of the two because there are medications that can slow your metabolic rate to the point where you absolutely appear to be dead. But the second part is going to be tricky. We'd have to find someone who is near death, someone who doesn't have friends or family ties, like perhaps a homeless person. But on top of that, he's going to have to be someone who's roughly your height, weight, and close to your physical features. That's an obstacle that will be a matter of opportunity. That could take obviously weeks, months, or even years.

"So more than likely, you're going to have to spend a long time waiting and being ready to go anywhere in the country on a moment's notice. I think you know as well as I do that there is no guarantee that you'll survive the freezing process. So if you're successful and you make it into the future, then in this timeline, I'll never know if you made it there or not because I will have died of old age by then. But if you make it there and you're unsuccessful, then I'll never see you again either way. But if you are successful and make it back, then in that new timeline, you and I will be the only ones who know about the other you...the frozen one!"

As he listened, Julian was rubbing the index finger of his right hand across his lips as his thumb rested on the bottom of his chin. He said, "You know, courage would be one thing. It's to do something that you don't have to do for the benefit of one or others, but this is something that I have to do. I have no choice. I've got to fix this." He stared straight forward for a long moment as his mind drifted toward negativity. "I'm going to miss out if I die or if I fail because I was going to get to know my old man. I got to meet him once, but I was going to get to know him. Now I may not have that chance, but if I don't try, then it will guarantee that there will never be a chance."

"Well, let's just focus on being positive. Your father is waiting for you there in the past. Just keep thinking to yourself that you're going to see him again. Now maybe you should head on back to Indiana and prepare yourself mentally and physically anyway you see fit, but just be ready when I make that call."

Chapter *9*

The Epiphany

Once Julian returned to Beech Grove, he felt that if he didn't survive or succeed in his mission that he should at least research as much as he could about his father. It would be the next best thing to being able to get to know him on a personal basis. He began doing so and found some surprising things. He started out discovering some small articles about his father's successes in local politics and then eventually moved on to the obituary. That led him to the newspaper article of the accident itself.

Julian began to feel cold and sick to his stomach as he read the report that said that his father had darted out in the street to shove a little boy out of the way of a speeding car and discovered that the little boy's name was... Drake Wallace!

He read that the four-year-old toddler named Drake Wallace had wandered into the road in pursuit of a rubber ball that he had dropped when his life was saved by the selfless actions of a heroic man named Gabe Phillips, who laid down his life to save the life of an innocent little boy. His mind was dizzy with the irony of this reversal of tragedy.

"No, no, no. This can't be. It can't be," he said aloud to no one. And then he immediately began to research the names of the parents of the toddler Drake Wallace. The file read, name of father unknown, but the name of the mother did match that of Drake Wallace. It was the same person. They were one in the same.

"No. Not my father." He yelled louder and louder. "Not my father! Not for that piece of shit!" As he stood up, he ripped the computer off the desk, smashing it against the wall and then grabbed the lamp and threw it through the window. He went on a rampage. He began tearing up the room, ripping his books off of their shelves, overturning his desk, doing everything he could do to get the rage out of him. He shouted, "Look at all that I have been robbed of so that you could live a life of debauchery!"

After destroying nearly everything he could get his hands on, he was scrunched down and huddled in the corner of the bedroom, exhausted but more from emotion than physical exertion. As he sat there in an upright fetal position, his curved and trembling hands vibrated about two inches in front of his face as he reviewed the tragedies of his life and focused his thoughts on the man who was at the center of it all.

He was steeped in hatred and anxiety but his misery was cut short by the ringtone of his cell phone. Shaking, he pulled the phone from his pocket and saw that the caller was James Daniel. He knew what this call meant, and a cold, steel look of revenge came over his face.

He answered the phone in a voice that was void of emotion, and without any courteous pleasantries, he just simply said, "Give me good news."

James said, "You've got it! You have to get down to New Orleans right away. There's a man from the French Quarter named Spinny Tapstau who's a homeless alcoholic, and he's dying from liver failure."

"His name is Spinny?"

"No. His real name is Spencer. Spinny is kind of a play on his name because of the way he staggers about when he's been drinking too much."

"Okay, how's this going to work?"

"Well, you're going to be greeted at the airport by two CIA operatives that will remain nameless. You see, I'm owed a favor for some unofficial business that we conducted on behalf of the CIA in the fight against terrorism."

"How will I know who they are?"

"They will know you. And they were aware of the UFO that was hovering above your house. They contacted me when that happened to get information on you. Though they didn't say anything more than that. It did coincide with the time frame you gave me about when you took that little ride. That's another reason I believed you."

Julian suddenly realized. "After I left your office, I was curious as to why you so readily believed me."

"Well, now you know. But anyway, after they greet you at the airport, they're going to take you to the Saint Tammany Parish Hospital and handle everything from there. And, Julian, with what little time you'll have, enjoy the warm weather of the South because you're going to be cold for a very, very long time."

"I'm ready and more than willing."

"Well, then get a move on because your plane leaves from the Indianapolis International Airport in right about two hours. There's a one-way ticket waiting for you at the Will Call just across from baggage claim near terminal D."

"Thanks, JD. Thanks for all of your help, and if I don't...if I don't—"

"Shut up, Julian. You will. Believe me you will. Now get going."

"All right. I'm gone."

For his departure, he prepared nothing. He packed nothing and brought no money to speak of. But he did make two pastrami and rye sandwiches with mustard. One, he would eat on the way to the airport. The other one, he left on the counter with a note that read, "Welcome Home."

When he arrived in New Orleans, he was greeted by the two men. They said very little and mainly just gestured in the directions they were heading. Once outside the airport, he was shuffled into a black limousine and whisked away. During the ride, he was debriefed by both of the operatives, each sitting on either side of him, the first one saying, "Your official new name from this point forward is Spencer Louis Tapstau."

The second one was saying, "A tax deferred annuity has been opened in your new name in the amount of one thousand dollars. By the time you are revived, you will be in California, and the amount of that annuity should accrue to approximately $130,000, enough to sustain you for a few months and include the price of a plane ride back to Indianapolis."

Then the other one said, "The duration of your cryogenic freezing will be a period of ninety-nine years and six months. At that point, we will all be dead except for you. Godspeed." The impersonal nature of their words left a lump in Julian's throat, and they said no more for the rest of the ride.

Once they arrived at the Saint Tammany Parish Hospital, he was greeted by another group of operatives who took him into a back entrance of the hospital that was cordoned off from the rest of the public. With uncertainty, he waited in a private room. A doctor or at least someone who appeared to be a doctor asked him to lay flat on the gurney table on which he was sitting. Rubbing alcohol was applied to the inner elbow area of his right arm, and the doctor said, "Just relax and count back from one hundred." As he pierced the needle into his vein, Julian began counting backward, "One hundred…ninety-nine…ninety-eight," and then he lost consciousness. Julian completely blacked out, and the procedure was underway.

He was then medically prepped for the freezing process, and his body was transported to the cryogenics lab in California where he would remain in a frozen stasis for the next ninety-nine years and six months. Julian's disappearance would soon become a national mystery, right up there with Jimmy Hoffa, Amelia Earhart, and the Lindbergh baby. A number of investigations (designed to go nowhere) would turn up, little more than a moldy pastrami sandwich covered in fruit flies.

The next sensation he would feel was intense pain through his entire body. He involuntarily began convulsing. He could not see, but he heard the muffled sound of someone say, "Get over here and help! This one's alive."

He heard another voice say, "How can that be? These patients were supposed to be dead when they were frozen."

He felt a number of hands holding down his legs and his arms as he shouted, "It hurts! God, it hurts. I can't see. I'm blind."

He heard a voice yell, "Prepare a mild anesthetic and get a counselor in here right away." The doctor then told Julian, "Be calm, be calm. Calm down. You're going to be all right. Your eyesight is going to come back in a couple of days. It's the last thing to be restored. Just be calm. We've got everything under control."

They applied heating pads, and the anesthetic began to take effect, and then a warm, soft, mother-ly-like voice said, "Be calm, Spencer. Be still. Everything will be okay. My name is Charlene, and I'm here to help you with the acclimation process."

* * * * *

Two days later, Julian was preparing to leave the hospital. The hospital was unreal. It was like nothing he'd ever seen before. Rather than televisions, there were crystal-clear holographic images. He was watching the news. The anchor was talking about how the colonies on Mars had, for the first time, topped a population of over 100,000 people.

I'll be damned. Looks like the Man on Mars project succeeded and without me? Now how can that be? he jokingly thought to himself.

Just then, Counselor Charlene Walker and Dr. William Halloran entered the room, and the doctor said, "Good morning, Spencer. How's the eyesight today? A little better than yesterday, I trust?"

"Yeah, just a little bit of blurriness left, but I guess that will clear up soon because it's a lot better than it was yesterday."

"That's normal, but they will be just fine in no time, and the rest of you is in tip-top shape, so I'm going to leave you in the capable hands of Charlene here. I've got more patients to see and little time to see them. He's all yours," he said as he looked at Charlene. Then looking back at Julian with a nod, he said. "Have a nice day, Spencer, and welcome to the future. I hope the transition goes smoothly for you."

"Thanks, Doc, I hope so too, time will tell." As Dr. Halloran left, Julian said to Charlene, "I'm kind of curious. It may be my eyesight, but you look like a pretty young woman, maybe twenty-five or thirty years old. But the other day when I really couldn't see at all, you said that you've been a counselor for twenty six years. How old are you?"

She laughed and said, "Advances in medical technology have slowed the aging process quite a bit, Mr. Tapstau. Actually, I just turned fifty."

He said with amazement, "Really? The future looks like a pretty amazing place."

She said, "Well, there are a few more technology toys than there were a hundred years ago. But one thing that hasn't changed since your day is world hunger. There are still a lot of people who are starving for no good reason. But that's conversation for another day. I'm here to finalize your release. Now, your new social-security number has already been affixed to your forehead and to the back of your right hand."

He looked down at the back of his hand and saw nothing. He looked back up at her with a curious face, and she said, "They're not visible to the human eye. They can only be seen with a special ultraviolet light. It's how you make purchases. Now, while the American dollar is still called the dollar, no one pays for anything with paper currency anymore. Whenever you buy something, that amount will automatically be deducted from your personal account. And your annuity has accrued to the amount of $143,252."

Julian said, "And no cents?"

She said, "Pardon me?"

"Change, I meant. I was joking."

"Oh, you mean coins like quarters, nickels, pennies, like that?"

"Yeah."

"No. Change is something that hasn't been used since before I was born." she said as she handed him something that looked like a credit card. "This pamphlet contains all kinds of social-program information to help you find employment and housing and so forth."

"It doesn't look like a pamphlet."

She said, "You simply insert it into any hologram station or computer, and it will automatically run through any piece of information that you need. And that's it. You're all set. All you have to do is sign out at the front desk before you leave, and if you need anything from me, my information is in that pamphlet."

"Okay. Thank you. Thank you very much. I think I'll be okay from here."

And then she said, "I've got one more thing to ask you. If you don't want to answer, it's okay. It's really none of my business, but it's something that's had us all curious for quite some time."

"What's that?" he asked.

"Well, you're not like all the rest we've revived. The reason most of the people who haven't been revived yet is because they've only had their cranium frozen, and the technologies for cloning as well as information transference isn't quite there yet and others because their cause of death hasn't reached medical treatability. Your condition, if you actually had it, would have been an easy fix many years ago, but our instructions were very specific when it came to you. You were to remain in a frozen stasis for ninety-nine years and six months. We were curious as to why. Also, once we revived you, there was no sign of liver failure."

Julian thought for a moment and said, "Let's just say I have a special purpose, and I'm not allowed to discuss it."

"Well, then the mystery for us continues, but, like I said it's none of my business, I suppose. Maybe I shouldn't have asked."

"No, I don't mind that you asked. It's just that I'm not at liberty to say. I think I've said enough already, and I pretty much have to get on my way. But thanks again."

Once leaving, he immediately made his way to LAX. The first thing that surprised him were the cars because there were no drivers. You simply got in, scanned the bar code on your hand, and spoke aloud where you wanted to go, and the car went there all by itself.

The structures of the buildings were amazing. The architecture was something straight out of a sci-fi film. And LAX was completely different than it had been before. It was a massive structure, many, many times larger than it had been. So were the airplanes. The average plane could hold over a thousand people. He realized his money wasn't going to last. His forty-minute car ride to the airport alone cost him just under $200 and the plane ride just over $5,000.

Once arriving in Indianapolis, it was another $120 cab ride to Beach Grove. The cab's computer didn't recognize any such location as Bobba Lou's since it no longer existed. He made a quick stop at an amazing space-age McDonald's where he ordered a Quarter Pounder with cheese, french fries, a small shake, and a large Coke. The total bill was a mere $57.

He found a dirty, run-down hotel to stay in, but he didn't mind because the price was right, only $2,700 for a one week stay. He had just over a month to wait, and he found the waiting was the hardest part. He calculated the amount of money he would need to sustain himself for that time period, including food, drink, room and board, and maybe a few changes of clothes. He figured if he played his money right, he would have approximately $119,000 leftover and he figured he would need every dollar if he failed to make it back to the past. He also thought maybe the night before confronting Drake, he would treat himself to a five-star meal in case it was his last.

In preparation for the long-awaited day, he researched and discovered the area where Bobba Lou's once stood, and Interstate 40 was now a superhighway that ran parallel about a block and a half to the south of where the old roadway once was. When he pinpointed the exact location, he found a number of old, burned-up planks of wood as well as scattered bricks and rubble, but it was difficult to determine where he was exactly on the old property. After careful inspection, he was eventually able to discern that which was once the back parking lot area, though trees and grass had grown through the old and broken pavement of what was now almost unidentifiable.

In the week that led up to the arrival of Drake, he returned every day at the exact same time to be certain that he did not miss his meeting with the self-appointed *God*. And then on the eve of that date with destiny, he made reservations for dinner at the prestigious Sanibel Cottage Restaurant and Event Center. His waiter introduced himself as Kevin, saying, "Are you dining alone, or are you waiting for someone?"

Julian replied, "I am indeed waiting for someone, but yes, I will be dining alone."

For Julian that evening, money would present itself as no object. Steak, lobster, and Château Lafite Rothschild would be the order of the day. Tomorrow he would either succeed, or he would likely die. And so it would be.

The next evening, as midnight approached, he was uncertain of which part of the once back parking lot the orb would appear. He kept his eyes peeled in every direction in anticipation of its arrival, and as each moment grew nearer, his heartbeat increased. His feet were tingling, like pins and needles of a body part that had fallen asleep. His hands were numb. Every fiber of his being was focused on this very moment.

He armed himself with an old tree branch that was about the length and girth of a baseball bat, even though he knew that he had the advantage of the groggy effects of time lag. It was still too important for there to be any misstep or any slip up at all. The hour was at hand, and the moment had arrived. Julian looked down at what was now his ancient timepiece known as a cell phone, and it clicked to midnight, but he saw and heard nothing.

"What's gone wrong?" he said to himself. "Come on...come on...rear your ugly head."

Those moments seemed to take forever. For Julian, it was as though another century had ticked by. He let out a worrisome exhale just as he heard the familiar electrical hum coming from behind him. He turned and looked and saw about thirty yards away; the metallic black orb had appeared.

He snarled as he ran, holding the tree branch over his right shoulder in a position ready to strike. The dazed and disoriented Drake saw Julian charging toward him, and like a drunk searching for his car keys, he attempted to hit the start button in hopes of escape. The misguided direction of his hand accidentally hit the return-time button, resetting it to April 20, one year prior to the date he departed. A second attempt would fare no better as Julian leveled a striking blow just beneath Drake's left shoulder, breaking his arm and knocking him clear of the time machine.

Julian was trembling from a combination of adrenaline and emotion as he grabbed Drake by the collar and dragged him about ten feet from the time machine. Julian was still holding the tree branch. As Drake attempted to sit up, Julian struck him again, this time across the teeth and nose. Blood spurted from his lip as he crashed back down to the ground. It was eerily similar to the attack Julian had suffered at the hands of Drake when the time machine was initially stolen. Drake was writhing in pain as he flailed about, much the way you would expect a blind man to if he were drowning.

"You need to die," Julian said. "I should crush your skull right now." And then he raised the tree branch above his head pointing skyward with both hands, looking down at Drake in preparation for a downward blow that would end his life.

But Julian couldn't do it. Even though he desperately wanted to, he just couldn't commit murder, even though Drake so richly deserved it. He couldn't bring himself to betray his own moral character. He threw the stick aside, returned to the time machine, sat down, and pondered. "I can't take him with me, and I can't leave him because he will kill again here in the future."

The bloody-faced Drake stood and charged toward Julian. With his broken left arm curled against his chest, he lunged at him with his right arm and hand extended. Julian, without a split second to spare, hit the start button, and the metallic orb appeared, severing the right hand of Drake, and it dropped to the bottom of the time machine as the beaten and now one-handed

Drake crashed to the rocky and broken, old pavement. It was now Julian who made it back safely but to the year prior to the original date that Drake had stolen the time machine. Disoriented and repulsed by the fleshy deposit next to his foot, he shovel kicked Drake's hand out of the time machine and into the parking lot of Bobba Lou's where it would soon be found, then he reset Spanky for one year plus six months to coincide with his cryogenic freezing.

He hit the start button and was off once again, this time returning to his own timeline. He arrived at his house just five minutes after when he left to fly out to Saint Tammany. Once he got into the house, he discovered the pastrami sandwich that he made and left uncovered on the kitchen counter prior to his departure to New Orleans, thinking to himself when he made it that if everything went well, the sandwich wouldn't even have time to get stale, and he was right. It was still fresh and delicious. He looked at the note written by the cryogenically destined version of himself and said, "Thanks for the welcome home my soon to be frozen friend!"

As he consumed the sandwich, he swizzled down an ice-cold Pepsi, all the while contemplating what to do about Drake. He couldn't just leave him there in the future to kill again. Or perhaps he bled out and didn't survive the encounter at all. *I can't risk it*, he thought, *because he may not die in the future, and I can't take that chance.* And then he had an epiphany, a moment of clarity. *I have a chance to make a difference, to benefit many, and I know now exactly what I must do.*

Chapter *10*

The Impact

Julian thought long and hard about where his role in history might lead, taking an entire week to mull it over in his mind before making his move. Now more determined than ever, he set off in the time machine, and he found himself there that sunny day at a street corner in the southeast of Indianapolis. He was there at the very time and place where his father had died at exactly 3:37 in the afternoon. There at the crosswalk was a cluster of people waiting to cross the street, and among them was his dad. He kept looking down and away so as not to be noticed by his father. Gabe was making small talk with potential supporters, one of them saying, "The words of a politician are cheap. It's the actions of a man that determine his worth."

"That's exactly why I ran for town council over in Beech Grove because so few engage in the words they say. Not bragging, mind you, but I've kept every campaign promise I made. I'm here to make a difference."

Julian knew that his father had only seen him that one time about two years prior to this timeline and didn't think he would recognize him, but he remained vigilant about being inconspicuous just in case. And then he saw the toddler Drake Wallace peering from behind the pantsuit of the woman who was in charge of him, and he began dividing his attention between his father who continued on with his political vision and the rubber-ball wielding young Wallace.

From Julian's perspective, time seemed to slow as the voices of the others seemed to carry into the background as he could hear more clearly the voice of the young Drake Wallace holding his red ball upward toward his caregiver, saying, "This is my ball, my ball. It's mine. It's my ball."

And also he heard the voice of his father saying, "People need to choose for themselves what they think is best and be allowed to decide from that what the course of their own lives should be."

And then the unspeakable happened when everyone's attention was turned to the left at the sound of a speeding car racing down the street pursued by a police car. It was a group of teenagers on a joy ride. But Julian, knowing the moment of reckoning was at hand, never took his eyes off his father. At that moment, the young Wallace dropped the rubber ball, and it struck the very edge of the curb, causing the ball to shoot directly into the road. The toddler darted after it saying, "My ball!" and his caretaker screamed, "Drakey, no!"

Gabe's reactionary instinct kicked in, and he sprang in the direction of Wallace. At the same time, Julian sprang in the direction of his father, tackling him from the side and knocking him safely to the sidewalk pavement. As they fell, Gabe let out a mournful scream, saying, "Nooo!" as the onlookers witnessed the horror of the car striking the toddler.

The car never even slowed down as the bone-crushing force of the impact was so great that Wallace was knocked clear of his shoes. The bloody and tattered body of the little boy lay about one hundred feet down the road.

As Julian rolled off to the side of his father and struggled to regain his feet, he pleaded in a blubbering and anguished voice, "God forgive me. God forgive me, please. God forgive me," as the gravity of what he allowed to happen to the innocent Drake overwhelmed him.

Gabe also regained his footing and shouted, "Why did you do that? Why did you stop me? I could have saved him!"

Julian, in a broken sob, yelled back, "Because you would have died!"

"What would it matter?" Gabe was gasping for breath. "He was a child!"

Julian, shaking, as though his nerves were set on fire, shouted, "IT MATTERS MORE THAN YOU KNOW, more than you'll EVER know!"

He backed away and then ran from the scene.

Chapter *11*

Everything I Ever Lost

A short time later, the time machine lay safely in the trunk of a taxicab as Julian made his way back to the old, familiar clearing in the woods near where he grew up. He was sitting in the back seat, and his face was pale and sweaty. The driver looked at him through the rearview and said, "Hey, bud, you going to be okay?"

Julian replied, "I don't know." Thoughts kept spinning in his head. *Did I do the right thing? Did I have another option?* He knew that if he held on to the arm of the young Drake that his father would have been safe, but he knew that as Drake grew, so would his thirst for killing. The chance that any of the lives Drake had taken before would be taken again, Julian felt he could not risk that. He felt as though he had no choice.

Once they arrived to where Julian had asked to be dropped off, the cabbie said, "That'll be $22.50 including tip." Julian pulled a gold coin from his pocket and flipped it at him. The driver took a look at it, pressed it to his teeth, and determined that it was the real thing. He looked back at Julian and said, "You realize that this is worth a lot more than the taxi ride here?"

And Julian said, "Time is money, and both are an illusion."

The cabbie said only one word, "What?" as though it were the dumbest thing he had ever heard.

Julian simply responded, "Never mind. Keep the change."

"Wow, thanks, man. This is the biggest tip I have ever had."

"Don't mention it."

Julian made his way into the woods and set up Pandora in the same spot that he had before, sat down, and thought to himself, *Who was I to play God?* And then he thought, *But then again, that's what Drake had been doing all along. It is what it is, and I can't change it now.* Then he paused and looked down at Spanky and hit the start button and returned to his own timeline.

As he was lugging the time machine, making his way up to the house, it was like seeing a ghost. It was Rebecca looking at him from the porch, and she shouted, "What are you doing out there? Playing Tom Sawyer or Huck Finn today?"

"Rebecca!" he shouted as he dropped the time machine and sprinted across the lawn.

"Calm down. What's wrong with you?"

He ran up to the porch and gave her the biggest and the longest hug, gasping as he held the back of her head. She said, "Take it easy, Julian. You act as though you haven't seen me in years."

Tears streamed down his face as he backed away from her slightly, holding both of her hands, and said, "Let me look at you. Let me look at you. You're healthy. You're so beautiful. You're just fine."

"Of course, I'm fine. We just had lunch. What's wrong with you, Julian?"

He noticed that she had a slight baby bump. He looked back up into her eyes and said, "You're pregnant."

"Of course, I am. And oh, by the way, I got the ultrasound back. We're having a girl this time!"

"This time?"

And just at that moment, his mother opened the door and stepped out onto the porch. "What's all the ruckus about?" she asked while holding a one-and-half-year-old little boy in her arms.

His whole body was trembling as he looked at her, nearly tripping as he darted over to give her a hug along with the little boy, saying, "Mom. Mama, you're okay… I mean, of course, you're okay. And this is my son. My son!"

And Rebecca said again, "What's wrong with you, Julian? Of course, he's your son. He's just like you. You're his hero."

And then from behind him out in the driveway, he heard someone calling out, "Air Force One is ready to go, President Phillips."

Julian turned and looked and saw two men dressed all in black. And farther behind them was an entire brigade of limousines. He looked back at his mother and his wife and said, "Who are they?"

And they both looked at each other and then back at Julian and said at the same time with a question mark, "Secret Service?"

His mother shouted back, "Give me a minute. I'll go and grab Gabe. He's probably on the phone with a king, a dignitary, an ambassador, or God only knows. Come on, Julian, come inside and get your things."

"Gabe?" he asked. "My father is here?"

"Julian, you're scaring me now. I'm going to seriously see about having you checked out."

And then his mother stepped back inside, and he followed in behind Rebecca as his mother shouted out that old, familiar call, "Gabe!"

His father emerged from the kitchen with three other Secret Service agents and what appeared to be a personal assistant, saying to them, "Look, if they're not willing to play ball, then I'm not willing to cross the aisle, and that's just the way it's going to be." He looked up at Julian and said, "What's going on, my boy?"

In a very low and shaken voice of disbelief, he said, "Dad?"

And his father responded jokingly, "That's Mr. President to you."

And in that instant in Julian's mind were picture-framed memories that he had never known before that began to flood in and emerge one at a time at the speed of light—himself as a toddler playing alone, now his father holding puppet animals in front of him, playing alongside of him. Another one again of himself at the local pool struggling to learn how to swim with his arm floaties, and now that memory merged with a new one, his father there with his hands underneath his stomach, holding him parallel to the surface of the water, encouraging him to stroke with his arms, then another of him standing outside the ball field, holding the fence with his hands as he looked on as the others played. Now his father as the coach, he was in center field, teaching him how to throw a ball.

All of the memories from the old and new timelines were now melding together side by side. The new memories were rushing in—the two of them riding next to each other in a golf cart on the way to the next hole, math homework, tennis lessons, how to ride a bike, how to drive a car, how to treat a lady and advice on his very first date, his graduation from high school and college, all with his proud father there. His marriage to Rebecca, and Gabe at the reception as the newly elected governor of Indiana, giving a powerful toast at the table of honor, the birth of their son Brandon, remembering the first time his son rolled over and his first steps, introducing his son to the world just as his father had for him. All of these memories now included his father and filled an enormous void in his life.

More than memory, he was instantly living each moment of a long-gone *new past*.

He looked around at his family as the new memories of the life that he had suddenly now lived, flooded into his mind. All the while there was a song blaring in his head. It was U2's "The Miracle."

> *"I woke up at the moment when the miracle occurred and the song that made some sense out of the world, everything I ever lost, now has been returned! The most beautiful sound I'd ever heard."*

He was overwhelmed by his new reality and fainted. When he came to, he was aboard Air Force One. The onboard doctor flickered a medical flashlight in his eyes saying, "Mr. President, we'll do a full checkup on him, but I don't think there's anything to worry about. His eyes are slightly dilated. By all accounts, I think it was just a combination of fatigue and an imbalance of electrolytes, but he should be just fine."

His father, Gabe, looked down at him and said, "Are you all right, boy?"

Julian looking up could see his father come into focus. He said, "It is you."

"It's me. Listen, I can't have you making any more headlines for me than I already have to deal with," he said with a chuckle.

After about twenty minutes or so and two cups of chamomile tea later, Julian remembered both timelines that he had lived up to that point and knew that he would be the only person who was aware of the old one. He also remembered full well all of his father's political history, moving up through the ranks, first as a town-council member, then mayor, then governor, and then the presidency.

Knowing that the last conflict in the Middle East never happened, he asked his father, "How did you avoid yet another Gulf War?"

His father said, "It's actually more simple than it is complicated."

"How so?"

"Well, the fact of the matter is that terrorists see compromise as weakness, and the more you compromise, the more they think they're succeeding. So they double down and fight even harder and recruit faster. If you show no mercy and no tolerance, you can at least keep them at bay. It's brutal, but it's effective, and it spares the lives of many more in the long run."

Julian thought about his decision to allow the innocent child to die but then remembered Drake's own thought that if Hitler died as a baby, he would be in heaven now. He thought surely that must be the same for Drake because of how many lives Drake now had not taken, including Janet Barnes who graduated from MIT and went on to have a successful career as well as five children and the other lives that now were not taken by Drake who had offspring of their own who never would have, who now had the chance to know love and happiness and not only them but also his entire family reunited as one, along with countless untold numbers of the military.

He had not only changed the course of history for himself but also for that of an entire nation and perhaps the world.

The end.